The
Penultimate Chance Saloon

The
Penultimate Chance Saloon

Simon Brett

THORNDIKE
WINDSOR
PARAGON

This Large Print edition is published by Thorndike Press®, Waterville, Maine USA and by BBC Audiobooks Ltd, Bath, England.

Published in 2006 in the U.S. by arrangement with The Toby Press, LLC.

Published in 2006 in the U.K. by arrangement with The Toby Press.

U.S. Hardcover   0-7862-8854-X (Core)
U.K. Hardcover 10: 1 4056 1496 X (Windsor Large Print)
U.K. Hardcover 13: 978 1 405 61496 2
U.K. Softcover 10: 1 4056 1497 8   (Paragon Large Print)
U.K. Softcover 13: 978 1 405 61497 9

The text of this Large Print edition is unabridged.
Other aspects of the book may vary from the original edition.

Set in 16 pt. Plantin by Al Chase.

Printed in the United States on permanent paper.

British Library Cataloguing-in-Publication Data available

Library of Congress Cataloging-in-Publication Data

Brett, Simon.
    The penultimate chance saloon / by Simon Brett.
      p. cm. — (Thorndike Press large print core)
    ISBN 0-7862-8854-X (lg. print : hc : alk. paper)
    1. Dating (Social customs) — Fiction.   2. Older men —
Fiction.   3. Reporters and reporting — Fiction.   I. Title.
II. Series: Thorndike Press large print core series.
PR6052.R4296P46 2006
823′.914—dc22   2006013699

To the lovely
— but sadly late —
Susan Hill,
with whom I discussed the idea
of writing a Gaga Saga

Chapter one

. . . and, by way of contrast, a woman in Cardiff divorced her husband on the grounds that he never went anywhere with her. He was not present at the hearing.

One of the great discoveries of humankind is post-menopausal sex — the love that dares not speak its name terribly loudly when younger people are present. The thought of wrinkled and wizened bodies engaging in that kind of activity is repellent . . . until, of course, it's your body that's wrinkled and wizened. Then entirely different values apply.

So Bill Stratton found out, when, on the verge of his sixtieth birthday, his wife Andrea left him for another man.

They had had what he would have described as a happy marriage. Only when Andrea spelled out, in great detail, her reasons for leaving him, did he realise that he was alone in that view.

They were different, he'd always known that, and if ever interviewed on the subject — as he occasionally had been — he would have said that the very differences between them were what made their marriage strong. Andrea's view, he subsequently discovered, had been at variance with his for quite a long time. Since the second week of the honeymoon, according to her, but he thought she was exaggerating. Surely, he'd said, it's not possible to spend nearly forty years married to someone you're convinced is the wrong person. Andrea assured him that it was entirely possible.

Her main criticism of him was that he was shallow. He took this on board to some extent, but he reckoned he probably wasn't deep enough to understand it fully. He had, after all, virtually made a career out of triviality.

Bill Stratton had been mildly famous, and he'd had a fairly easy ride. Having found his mild fame as a television newsreader, he had never been under the illusion that this was a particularly taxing role in life. His looks were good enough (in spite of a slightly crooked smile), his personality was amiable enough, and he had the ability to deepen his voice and look as if he was really suffering when there was a disaster to announce.

He had even gained the vacuous honour of a catchphrase. The news editors of his day were keen to end their bulletins on a light note, and would trawl the international media for amusing snippets, which Bill Stratton would introduce with a wry smile, followed by his trademark, 'and, by way of contrast . . .' The phrase increased his recognition factor, and developed some surprisingly lucrative spin-offs.

Never did Bill attempt to dignify his profession by claiming that it had any great importance in the scheme of things, or brought any particular benefit to humanity. On forms he put down his profession as 'Journalist' — and even had an NUJ card to prove it — but he knew that what he did could not really be dignified by the name of journalism. He just read an autocue. Someone had to do the job, and he was the lucky guy who'd got it.

The rewards were extraordinarily generous, given the amount of effort involved. There had been a stage, early in his career, when he had tried to justify his employers' largesse to earnest friends of Andrea (and Andrea didn't have any friends who weren't earnest). He'd said he was paid for the responsibility, for what might happen if terrorists took over the studio while he was live on air, an eventuality for which he had to be ready at all times. But he soon gave up. The argument wasn't even convincing him, and given that all Andrea's earnest friends worked at some level of the National Health Service, he knew, when it came to moral high ground, he hadn't got a leg to stand on. Besides, his was not a particularly strong character. He knew if terrorists did take over the studio while he was live on air, he would abjectly read out any demands or manifestos they told him to.

Bill Stratton was by nature obedient. He had a sense of duty. This wasn't spontaneous, but had been inculcated into him by a strong mother and a minor public school education. There were things that you should do, and things that you shouldn't do. He had been born just too early for his adolescence to be much affected by the sixties, when a lot of the things you shouldn't do became things you should do. Growing up in a provincial town, for Bill the excesses of Carnaby Street were the stuff of newspapers and news bulletins. He didn't see any evidence of a new liberalism in the people around him. The Swinging Sixties were supposed to be happening, but like many potentially exciting things in his life, they seemed to be happening somewhere else.

At nineteen, while studying history and politics at a university that did not aspire to dreaming spires, he had met Andrea, who was training at a nearby nursing college. They had got on well, they had wanted to go to bed together, so they had announced their engagement. That, Bill knew, was what a young couple in their situation should do. And their wedding was duly solemnised the autumn after his graduation.

Though not technically virgins when they married, they might as well have been. Neither had much sexual experience, certainly little with anyone else. And the marriage, like a new plant, bedded down very satisfactorily. At least in Bill's view.

But not, apparently, in Andrea's. Again, he found himself trying to counter disbelief when the fifty-eight-year-old Andrea asserted that their sex life had never been satisfactory. How could two people maintain such different views of something in which they were so intimately involved?

What she said about children had been a bit of a body-blow too. Bill had assumed, as month by month no signs of pregnancy occurred, that they were just one of those couples who couldn't have children. The lack gave him the occasional pang, but he wasn't really that bothered. He'd never been one of those men desperate for the continuity of his genes, and he didn't actually find children very interesting.

He had assumed that the lack of offspring might have been more hurtful for Andrea, but she very rarely mentioned the subject. So he, not wishing to stir emotional pain, didn't either. To Bill there seemed nothing wrong with their childless state. Indeed, it brought many positive benefits. They were better-off, and could enjoy many freedoms denied to their progeny-hampered friends.

So he received another shock when, in one of Andrea's parting speeches, she assured him that, for as long as it had been necessary throughout their marriage, she had used contraception. She had decided, apparently in the second week of the honeymoon. (What a momentous week that had clearly been for Andrea; how could he have been so completely unaware of what had been going through her mind at the time?) Anyway, she told him that she had decided in the second week of their honeymoon that, though she wanted children, she did not want to have Bill Stratton's children. Which, when he thought about it, wasn't very flattering.

She said a lot else, too — much of which he was happy to let slip into oblivion down the Teflon sides of his brain. Sometimes being shallow had its advantages.

Andrea had believed in the principle of

marriage as much as Bill had. She too sub-
scribed to the 'should' theory of human ob-
ligations. She didn't believe that a marriage
ought to be abandoned just because it was
imperfect. Like everything else, marriage
had to be 'worked at' and it would get
better. This attitude was central to her
training as a nurse. In order to do her job,
she had to continue in the conviction that
her patients would ultimately get better,
even though the long-term evidence did not
support that view.

Bill had always been more cynical about
such matters, but he didn't share his opinions with his wife. The world needed people
with her attitude, and was a better place
with Andrea in it. No point in making her
question the foundations of her positive approach.

Between husband and wife there was, at
bottom, an ideological divide. Andrea had
always believed the world was improvable.
Bill had never really thought that. The
world, he knew, was an irredeemable mess,
and it was down to the individual — or at
least to Bill Stratton — to make the best out
of that depressing situation.

His rationalisation of the differences between them came in the wake of Andrea's
leaving him. That shock prompted a lot of

rationalisation. Though Bill Stratton's nature was not given to introspection, in the stunned weeks after her departure he indulged in more self-analysis than he had in the rest of his lifetime.

He tried to work out what had gone wrong. More than that, he tried to work out why he hadn't noticed that anything had gone wrong. There must have been signs of Andrea's discontent. And yet, if her disillusionment dated from as early in the marriage as she claimed, he had probably interpreted those signs simply as expressions of her personality. Yes, she was grumpy at times. So was he. Everyone was grumpy at times. Yes, she sometimes snapped at him. Ditto.

Then why had it gone wrong? Soul-searching was an unfamiliar exercise to Bill Stratton, and he found it intriguing as well as painful. He was also suitably modest about his soul-searching potential. The world, he knew, was full of people with souls as deep as the deepest oceans, whose exploration required the services of an emotional bathysphere. He reckoned for searching his own soul a shrimping net would probably be adequate.

He tried to identify where in the marriage he might have been at fault . . . apart from just by being shallow. Shallowness was in his nature — he couldn't do much about that — but he liked to think he had shown a proper interest in Andrea's more serious pursuits. He had listened at great length and with apparent attention to bulletins about the fluctuating health of her patients. He had nodded sympathetically and continuously when she and her friends had bewailed the shortcomings of the National Health Service and their line managers.

He didn't think he'd imposed his own wishes too forcibly on his wife. Granted, in the early years of their marriage, he had been perhaps a little too assertive in the matter of holidays. His idea of bliss — an uneducated idea, he subsequently came to recognise — was a hotel on a Mediterranean shore with easy access to swimming pools, bars and restaurants. Only after three such holidays had Andrea made clear to him that she didn't enjoy spending time in 'tourist traps, which gave an unreal and completely sanitised impression of what the life of the country was really like.'

To give himself his due, Bill had responded. From then on, he'd allowed Andrea to select their holiday destinations and, in the cause of avoiding 'tourist traps', had suffered diarrhoea in most countries of

15

the Third World. He had expressed appropriate interest in herbal remedies, mud baths and rebirthing rituals. As a result, though he'd felt intermittently virtuous, he'd never had much fun on holidays. But he had always thought he was behaving rather well as a husband, letting his own wishes be subservient to those of his wife.

In fact, he would have said he'd done that in most areas of their marriage. But evidently he hadn't done so enough to satisfy Andrea. He tried to think what other deficiencies he had as a human being. And he could only really come up with two major ones.

First, he had never been very pro-active; he rarely made things happen but was always quite happy for them to happen to him.

And, second, Bill Stratton suffered from that commonest and most debilitating of human failings — the desire to be liked.

Inevitably, as he trawled the shallows of his soul during this post-break-up period, sex arose, a huge bristling obvious lobster amidst the surrounding transparency of shrimps. Sex, Bill Stratton knew, from reading such unimpeachable authorities as the *Daily Mail*, was what made and broke marriages.

Well, he'd thought their sex life had been

16

all right. Maybe more vigorous and frequent in the early years, but that was only to be expected. The attraction seemed to remain, and impotence was rare and usually alcohol-induced. They certainly weren't one of those couples from the *Daily Mail*, whose 'marriage was a sham' or 'a marriage only in name'. Even when they reached fifty, Bill and Andrea Stratton still made love a couple of times a week, and it was fine. Absolutely fine. Though if Bill had been asked the next morning whether they had made love or not the night before, he might have had to think about it.

Granted . . . the frequency of intercourse had rather dropped off in their early fifties, but that was due to the menopause. At least, Andrea said it was due to the menopause and, like most men, Bill Stratton was too squeamish to ask for further details.

Being an only child, he had grown up in a house where his mother was the only woman, and the idea of her discussing the mystery of women's bodies with him had been unthinkable. The idea of his father discussing the subject with him was even more far-fetched, and the idea of his father discussing such matters with his mother was beyond the scope of conjecture.

As a result, the two 'm's — menstruation

and menopause — had remained unmentioned in the Stratton household. In common with most children, to the young Bill the idea of his parents having an active sex life was distastefully unimaginable. When he was sixteen, at the time of maximum hormonal confusion, the idea of people of thirty having an active sex life was unimaginable (almost as unimaginable then as the idea of he himself ever getting to the point of having a sex life).

But Bill Stratton's adolescent gleanings of incomplete information had left him with the firm conviction that the menopause definitely closed the lid down on all that stuff. If grown-ups hadn't had the decency to stop having sex before, at least the menopause would put a permanent end to their little games. Post-menopausal women would become little old ladies, like his grandmothers.

Better information gathered through his life should have dissipated this illusion. The media — particularly the *Daily Mail* — were increasingly loaded with over-frank testimonials from mature women about their continuing and flowering sexuality — but Bill was never quite convinced. The primitive beliefs of his childhood had left their imprint on his thinking. His image of the menopause remained as a big, dark, heavy shutter.

As a result, when Andrea told him the menopause had caused her to lose interest in sex, he was disappointed, but not surprised. And, to his mind rather nobly, he did not force his attentions on her. His libido was not as rampant as it had been, and, wistfully, he tried to reconcile himself to the fact that that part of his life might be over.

He was therefore not a little upset when Andrea told him the real reason she had stopped having sex with him was nothing to do with her time of life. That, rather than diminishing it, the menopause had increased her enjoyment of sex.

Sex with someone else.

He was called Dewi, which to Bill seemed only to add insult to injury. If he was going to have a love rival, at least he could have been granted one with a less silly name.

But he had to admit that her new man's profile was perfect for Andrea. A doctor throughout his career, Dewi Roberts had resisted the attractions of even the minimum of private work and devoted all of his professional life to the NHS. He had also volunteered much of his spare time for committee work, and had travelled extensively taking medical help to the world's impoverished peoples. Dewi was so worthy he made Bill want to puke.

Nor could this paragon be criticised for the seduction and abduction of Andrea. Dewi was not betraying anyone, his wife having died of emphysema five years before their meeting, leaving him with three children, all of whom were at university studying worthy subjects. He was devoted to his offspring, and, though he and Andrea were mutually in love, had insisted for a long time that it would 'be better' if they stopped seeing each other. Dewi didn't want to have the break-up of her marriage on his conscience.

It was then, Andrea related to Bill with perhaps excessive glee, that she had told Dewi her relationship with her husband was 'a sham' and 'a marriage only in name'. Now she had met the right person, all she wanted to do was to divorce Bill and 'make up for lost time'. She also wanted to 'get to know' Dewi's children and 'build up a relationship with the next generation that had been denied to her throughout her unfulfilled marriage'.

Andrea's logic and determination were difficult to argue with, and Bill didn't try that hard. When she was that clear about what she wanted to do, he knew from experience that there was little point in trying to dissuade her.

So, unwillingly but with as much good grace as he could muster, he bit the bullet and agreed to the divorce. Andrea said that was 'the best present he had ever given her', a phrase that did not fill him with delight. And she wasted no time in walking back from the altar as the new Mrs Roberts.

So there Bill Stratton was, very nearly sixty, and no longer married. And, despite having had a continuous supply for nearly forty years, he had very little experience of sex. One premarital fumble with someone else, and then wall-to-wall Andrea. He knew that men tended to be more numerical than women about such things, but he couldn't help counting. At the end of his marriage, Bill Stratton's score of women made love to was . . . two. Well, no, thinking back to that premarital fumble, to be accurate it was one and a half. Actually, to be *generous,* it was one and a half.

And he had no idea whether, at the end of his life, that would be 'Latest Score' or 'Result'. But he'd be interested to find out.

During the period of the break-up and divorce Bill Stratton had felt many emotions,

most of them new, and most of them un-
pleasant. The one he hadn't felt at any time,
though, was guilt.

Chapter two

. . . and, by way of contrast, a Mr Ablethorpe of North Yorkshire has named his dog 'Mrs Ablethorpe', saying, 'It's been a darned sight more comfort to me that my wife ever was.'

Married friends of a marriage have to be very even-handed. Conversations between couples in cars leaving after evenings spent with the marriage may be more honest, but in its presence the illusion has to be maintained that both members of each couple like each other equally. When a marriage falls apart, that convention also breaks down. That's when you really find out who your friends are.

You also lose a lot of friends. Couples herd together in their detached pens like sheep, disproportionately paranoid at the idea of lone wolves prowling. A woman who, in the company of her husband at a dinner party, was cancelled out and anonymous, becomes, having shed the marital encumbrance, a potent threat to the integrity of coupledom. After one token invitation to show sympathy, she is quickly excised from the couples' dinner party list.

A recently unshackled man fares better. He gets invited out more, though not so much by the couples he used to visit with his former wife. Invitations arrive from people he didn't think he knew. An unattached man in an urban area is like an expanding ladder or a petrol-driven garden strimmer — sooner or later everyone's going to want to borrow it.

In the fall-out of Bill and Andrea Stratton's marriage, the division of friends was predictable, working out pretty much on career lines. Those with medical connections gravitated automatically to the new Mr and Mrs Roberts. As a conversationalist, Dewi could add so much more than Bill's sympathetic nodding. He could actually contribute his own experiences of the National Health Service's shortcomings, and whinge along with the best of them.

As for Bill, he found himself still in touch with most of his media connections. This suited him well. Gossip of journalism and show business seemed incontestably more interesting than maundering on about the Trust status of hospitals, and he was genuinely amazed when, in one of her tirades building up to the split, Andrea had announced how bored she had been at 'endless evenings of D-List celebrity trivia'. Could she really be serious?

So Bill still had his professional circuit of friends. His social life with them involved less dinner parties, more meeting at public events, launches, awards ceremonies and so on. Conversations with such people rarely rose above amiable banter, which suited Bill extremely well. And he had a few closer friendships with a variety of individuals, whom he would meet intermittently for lunch. Andrea's social life — and, by extension, his while they were still married — had been more to do with seeing the same small circle of friends time and time again.

Bill's was also less couple-oriented . . . particularly because the coupling and uncoupling amongst his media associates was more frequent than it had been with Andrea's NHS friends. Bill's divorce made little impression on his group of casual acquaintances. Few of them had been aware that he'd ever been married.

The one person with whom he was surprised to find himself still in touch was Ginnie Fairbrother. Although she worked in the theatre, he had always thought of Ginnie as Andrea's friend. That went back a long way. The two girls had known each other at boarding school and, even through the wide divergence of their careers, had stayed in touch. Andrea had gone to nursing college, Ginnie to drama school.

When Bill had become a permanent part of Andrea's life, Ginnie had become an intermittent ingredient in his. She would disappear for long periods, months away touring, filming or enjoying increasingly high-profile love affairs, but she'd always come back to share her experiences over the pine kitchen table of the Stratton's Putney home.

Bill was very happy with this arrangement, which guaranteed him the continuing company of an undoubtedly attractive woman. Had he not been married, Virginia Fairbrother would have been way out of his league. But the coincidence of her having his wife as a childhood friend gave Bill Stratton unembarrassed access to this exotic creature. Their relationship had always encompassed a level of flirtatiousness, which Andrea, knowing how entirely safe she was, mildly encouraged.

Ginnie had also proved useful to Bill on a professional level. There were occasionally receptions or award ceremonies which Andrea couldn't make, because she had some pressing hospital commitment (though, knowing what he did after the break-up, Bill wondered whether some of these had been fictitious). And if Ginnie also happened to be free, she would often accompany him to these events. They enjoyed each other's company, they could share giggles at the display of egos around them, and generally have a good relaxed time.

Given Virginia Fairbrother's blossoming fame and Bill Stratton's own mild celebrity, their presence together sometimes prompted the tabloids to speculations of steamy romance. Neither of them minded the insinuations — they did their images no harm — but both thought the fact that they were made was hilarious.

Despite their empathy, Bill had still always thought of Ginnie as Andrea's friend. He was therefore surprised when, as the tsunami of the divorce was receding, on one of the first nights he spent in his new flat, he received a telephone call from Virginia Fairbrother.

'I've no idea where you are,' said the voice-over which had sold everything from anti-ageing cream to annuities, 'but I thought there was a strong chance you'd still have the same mobile number.'

'As you see, you were right. Really good to hear you, Ginnie.'

'So how're you enjoying your resurrection as a single man?'

'Quite honestly, I haven't had time to think about it. There's been so much practical stuff to do. Selling the big house, getting this place . . .'

'Which is where?'

'Pimlico. Two-bedroomed, according to the estate agent, but the whole lot would fit into the kitchen in Putney.'

'Still, very sensible to move closer to the centre.'

'You think so?'

'Definitely.'

'Good.'

The conversation was becalmed for a moment. Bill knew they had soon to get on to the subject of Andrea — not to mention Dewi — but he was in no hurry. He wanted to prolong the glow engendered by Ginnie ringing him.

But it was she who broke the impasse. 'I think we should meet for dinner, Bill.'

He thought that was an excellent idea.

Inevitably, it was a new place. Someone like Virginia Fairbrother was a barometer of aspiring London restaurants. She knew where to be seen, and knew how important her being seen in the same place twice might be to the venture's success. Although she'd never been there before, the well-muscled greeter recognised her, took her to the appointed table and made no demurral when she asked for somewhere less central.

The decor was all cream plastic and stainless steel tubing — laboratory chic. The asymmetrical white crockery and thin cutlery maintained the image of kidney bowls and scalpels.

'I wouldn't give this one very long,' said Ginnie, as she settled into a screened plastic booth, which might have been designed for the production of specimens.

'No,' Bill agreed, half expecting privacy curtains to be wheeled across the opening. 'Still, I suppose its survival will depend on what the food's like.'

Ginnie shook her head firmly. 'With a couple of totally brilliant exceptions, most London food is of a good enough average standard these days. No, what matters to a place like this is what it looks like, and . . .' she cast her discriminating eye around the room '. . . who comes.'

She gave a little wave to a former soap star who'd unwillingly died of cancer three months previously, and a footballer whose career as a pundit had been curtailed by his total inability to stop himself from swearing onscreen.

'No, I wouldn't think it'll be long,' she confirmed.

'Well, you're here, Ginnie. That must give the place a lift.'

She reached across the table and gave his hand an appreciative rub. 'Sweet of you to say so, darling, but I don't think I'm quite the level they need. Afraid my wrinkles are starting to join together and shape up into a sell-by date.'

Bill Stratton went to great lengths to assure Virginia Fairbrother how inaccurate her self-assessment was, and he meant it. When Andrea had first introduced him to her, Ginnie had been tall and thin, with striking red hair. She was still tall and thin, with striking red hair, though presumably — Bill wasn't really up on such female secrets — the redness was now expertly assisted. That evening it was worn in relaxed curls, pulled back off her face with that artlessness which can only be achieved through extremely expensive artifice. The face itself, always sharp-featured, had not relaxed into fat; rather the years had tightened and burnished it like a much-polished bronze. Her skin glowed from a recent week's filming in the Mediterranean, and

Virginia Fairbrother was far too skilled an operator for there to be any indication where the make-up stopped and the tan started.

And yes, there were wrinkles, a fine tracery of lines which tightened and proliferated when she grimaced or smiled (and, being an actress, she grimaced and smiled a lot). But Bill Stratton's eyes found nothing ugly in the wrinkles; they defied blandness and infused character into the famous face.

Of course, Ginnie knew how to dress too. The hair and tan were set off by chunky matt brass jewellery: earrings, a choker and an incomplete circle on her thin wrist. The dress, shin-length to show enough tanned leg, was in some ruched cotton material the colour of dried blood.

Virginia Fairbrother looked stunning. But then she'd devoted her entire life to looking stunning.

They ordered gin and tonics and consulted the menu. At least the medical theme wasn't carried through there: no entries for Dialysis of Devilled Kidney or Roast Hip Replacement of Lamb. Ginnie — and Bill, following her example — made their selections quickly and gave the order to a waiter with an unfeasibly small bottom.

'No,' said Ginnie, looking round the ward, 'I don't think this place'll last long.'

31

She raised her glass. 'Cheers.' They clinked. 'So . . . how does it feel, Bill?'

'How does what feel?'

'Being single. Being free. Having the world as your oyster.'

He let out a sardonic laugh. 'Ginnie, I'm pushing sixty.'

'So what?' She leant close, engulfing him in a perfume far too expensive to have a name. 'Breathe this in the hearing of a tabloid journalist and I will personally castrate you, but . . . I'm pushing sixty too.'

He was taken aback. 'Pushing sixty-two?'

Virginia Fairbrother's mouth tightened into a little ring of disapproval. 'No. Pushing sixty *as well*. "Too" in the sense of "as well".'

'Ah. Right.'

'Come on, I can't pretend with you. You know I was Andrea's contemporary at school.'

'True.'

'Anyway, what is this, Bill? I don't think of you as a depressive.'

'No, I'm certainly not.'

'You always seem to have had a reasonably sunny outlook on life.'

'Yes, I think I have.'

'You certainly needed it, married to Andrea.'

A moment of disloyalty. Ginnie would never have said that while they'd still been together. Bill noted the lapse, but didn't pick up on it. Time enough to find out how much more disloyalty Ginnie might be capable of. But the moment gave him a little frisson. It opened up the possibility of criticising Andrea.

But for the time being, though, he concentrated on his age. 'I just feel, being sixty —'

'You're not sixty yet.'

'Near as makes no difference. So I've had my career — that's over . . .'

'Not entirely.'

'Again, near as makes no difference. I've had my marriage — that's over. I need to rethink.'

'Emotionally?'

'What do you mean?'

'Do you need to rethink what your emotional needs are . . . in your new circumstances?'

'All right. Yes, I suppose I do.'

'Then you also have to think about what kind of woman will fulfil those needs.'

'Ginnie, I have just come through a . . . I was going to say "long and painful divorce", but I know, compared to some people, I've got off relatively lightly. But it still has been quite traumatic, and the last thing I need at the moment is to remarry.'

'Who's talking about remarrying? You don't have to marry every woman you have a relationship with.'

'No, I know I don't, but . . .'

'You sound almost as if you think you do.'

Bill Stratton assessed this claim and found, to his great discomfort, that it wasn't far from the truth. In the late sixties he'd thought you had to marry someone with whom you wanted to have a relationship. Hence his wedding to Andrea. And, though he now knew the idea was as outdated as his concept of the menopause, he couldn't deny that, somewhere in the recesses of his mind, its vestigial presence remained.

'Andrea told me,' Ginnie went on, characteristically direct, 'that you were completely faithful to her throughout your marriage.'

'So?' He didn't want to commit himself to a confirmation of that yet. Wait and see the direction in which the conversation was moving.

But Ginnie's next words suggested she didn't need confirmation. 'I was always surprised you didn't have affairs, Bill.'

'Why should I have done?'

'Because you're an attractive man, and clearly everything wasn't right with your marriage.'

'I didn't realise there was anything wrong with my marriage until Andrea told me there was.'

'Oh, come on. I know for a fact that you hadn't made love for eighteen months before you split up.'

He couldn't deny the fact, but he wondered how she knew, and he also wondered which other of his bedroom secrets Ginnie was privy to. He felt one of his gender's recurrent anxieties: what do women talk about when we're not there?

'Surely you must have resented the lack of sex?'

'Yes,' he conceded.

'Then why on earth did you put up with it?'

Bill wasn't about to give a straight answer to that. If he hadn't been able to talk to his own wife — ex-wife, now — about the menopause, he certainly wasn't going to talk to another woman about it. But even as he had the thought, he realised that Ginnie must know about the subject. Must by then have gone through her own menopause — quietly, or uncomfortably, or melodramatically. Once again he was aware of the unbridgeable gulf between the male and the female experience.

'Well,' he fudged. 'Andrea didn't seem keen . . .'

'She didn't seem keen on making love to you because she was screwing like a rabbit with . . . whatever his name is . . . Huey, Dewey or Louie?'

'Dewi,' Bill corrected, pronouncing the name to rhyme with 'Bowie', in the approved Welsh manner.

'I think you've got a lot of ground to make up,' Ginnie announced firmly.

'On what?' asked Bill, genuinely puzzled.

'Sex, you fool.'

'Ah.'

Fortunately perhaps, further immediate discussion was halted by the arrival of their starters. Everything was wilted or drizzled in a marginally old-fashioned way. Ginnie poked at hers. 'No, I don't think I will be coming back here again.'

The waiter with the unfeasibly small bottom handed over to a waiter with a slightly more feasible bottom, who performed an elaborately choreographed wine-bottle-opening routine. By the time that was concluded, Bill hoped the conversation would have moved on. But Ginnie was determined not to let it.

'When did you actually marry Andrea?' she asked. 'I know I was there, but I've forgotten the exact date.'

'11th December, 1967.'

'And had you had much sexual experience before that?'

Bill poked his scalpel at something wilted in his white kidney bowl. 'Not much,' he mumbled.

'And you really were never unfaithful to her while you were married?'

He shook his head, aware of his colour rising.

'Why not?'

'I don't know. It's just . . . well, if you're married, you should be faithful, shouldn't you?'

'Yes, you *should*,' Ginnie conceded, 'but we're only *human*.'

Bill shrugged, again hoping that the conversation would move on.

It still didn't. 'Don't you think you missed something, Bill?'

'What?'

'Experience? Variety? I mean, by getting married so young?'

'I don't know. It felt right at the time. Andrea and I thought that's what we should do.'

'Back to "should" again. "Should" seems to have been a dominant impulse in your life.'

'Maybe.'

'So you missed "The Summer of Love" . . .' She managed to imbue the words with a throaty nostalgia, a memory of much-enjoyed excesses.

'Yes. Apparently there was a sexual revolution going on, but Andrea and I got nowhere near the barricades.' He couldn't completely exclude a tinge of wistfulness from his voice.

Then, as he often did when he wanted to change the course of a conversation, he remembered a line from his professional past. 'Actually, there was a rather good "by way of contrast" snippet about the sexual revolution. A man in Sidcup —'

But Ginnie was not to be diverted. 'I don't want to hear about that. I want to discuss what we're going to do about your sex life.'

'Nothing to discuss. I don't have one.'

Facetiousness wasn't going to deflect her either. 'That, Bill darling, is exactly what we want to discuss.'

And she fixed her hazel eyes on him so piercingly that he had to look away.

'Look, I can't recreate the sixties in the

twenty-first century.'

'Why not?'

'Because I'm actually *in* my sixties.'

'Not yet.'

'Near as damn it.'

'Well, I think you could have a very good time, Bill. You're attractive, witty, still got your hair . . .'

'White, though.'

'Doesn't matter for a man. No, you're going to enjoy yourself.'

'Maybe in time. Right now, I'm still pretty shell-shocked after the divorce.'

'Are you really?'

Again the hazel eyes seemed to bore through to the core of truth within him and, though he assured her of the genuine nature of his emotions, he wondered how honest he was being. In fact, now that the practical details of the divorce had been sorted, he thought very little of Andrea. Tucked away in a large house in Muswell Hill, comforted by Dewi and by constant phone calls from his worthy children, she had become a person in another life. And nearly forty years of marriage had the residual impact of a brief meeting.

Bill still felt the need to talk about other things, so he moved on to the one subject that, over the pine kitchen table in Putney, had been an infallible conversation-deflector. 'Anyway, how's *your* love life, Ginnie?'

She let out the long sigh that had held Chekhov audiences rapt at the National Theatre. 'As ever, darling. All my relationships are absolute hell.'

'And who are you giving hell to at the moment?'

'No one. It's just too painful to think of starting up with someone else. With each new relationship, the knowledge that it's going to end in tears kicks in nearer the beginning. I'm giving up sex,' she drawled, in a way that was incredibly sexy. 'Too old for it.'

Bill could have argued that that wasn't what she'd just been telling him, but didn't want to sabotage his successfully manoeuvred change of subject. So instead he listened with relish to Virginia Fairbrother's tales of her lovers, almost all of whom were high-profile actors, whom she deftly excoriated with waspish wit.

The evening passed in an amiable flurry of bitchiness. Although the dinner had been Ginnie's suggestion, Bill insisted on paying the bill. When her taxi arrived, and he dithered as to which cheek to peck first, he was surprised to find the softness of her lips pressed against his.

And that night, alone in his double bed in Pimlico, there were stirrings inside Bill Stratton's pyjama trousers of something he'd almost forgotten about.

Chapter three

. . . and, by way of contrast, a newsreader on a local television station in Indiana, who proposed to his girlfriend during a news bulletin, received fifty-four acceptances.

In semi-retirement, Bill Stratton was actually well-heeled. He was a member of the last generation whose pension arrangements looked likely to meet their post-career needs. His income had always been reasonably good — at times exceptionally good — and he had been able to salt away the maximum allowable percentage into pension funds.

And, unusually in such situations, he had profited from the divorce. Andrea had always had a dark secret, which she was at pains to keep from her right-on NHS friends: her parents had money. As a result, they had subsidised the young Strattons' first house purchase, thus putting them a few rungs above their contemporaries on the property ladder. This bonus, at a time when only the deeply stupid could fail to make money out of buying and selling houses, had increased exponentially with each subsequent move, until, by the time of the divorce, the value of the Putney house almost embarrassed Bill. It certainly embarrassed Andrea, so perhaps guilt was a factor in her ready agreement that the profits of the sale should be divided fifty-fifty between them.

The purchase of the Pimlico flat, lavish though it was, had still left Bill with a wodge of capital, which he had invested in an unspectacular but safe savings account. And his earnings potential had not died totally with his retirement from full-time newsreading. His agent, Sal Juster, rang him regularly with requests for minor presentation or personal appearance jobs. These were random and unsolicited, but Sal assured him that he had only to 'say the word', for her to start the positive marketing of Bill Stratton, which would bring a flood of new offers. And, she kept urging, he hadn't begun to explore the lucrative after-dinner speaking market. Bill found this knowledge a reassuring comfort blanket, but he hadn't as yet 'said the word'. In the surprisingly benign haze of his post-divorce life, he didn't want to rush into anything.

And then, of course, he still derived some income from BWOC.

This was the acronym of his catch-phrase, 'by way of contrast . . .', which, remarkably, had turned into a rather effective small business. At the time of his maximum exposure on the nation's news bulletins, Bill had been approached by an enterprising small publisher. If the best of the 'by way of contrast' sign-off stories were gathered into a small book, the entrepreneur suggested, they might make an attractive little package for the 'Christmas funny' market. Producing the book would not involve any work on Bill's part. The publisher's editor would contact the television company's researchers to find the content and knock it into shape. All Bill Stratton would be required to do was to give his name to the project, have his photograph — showing his famous crooked smile — taken for the front cover, and . . . the publisher was deeply apologetic for making this final outrageous request . . . write a two hundred and fifty word introduction to the book.

In return for these strenuous efforts, the book would be published as the work of Bill Stratton, he would receive a substantial advance and generous scale of royalty payments.

After a good nano-second of self-questioning, he agreed to take on the project.

Shortly before this offer, Bill had first been approached by Sal Juster, proposing that she should represent him. Regarding himself as a mere newsreader, he couldn't imagine that he'd ever need the services of an agent, but saw no harm in agreeing to her suggestion. Sal had taken on the *By Way of Contrast* book as their first mutual project and, to prove how valuable she would be to her client in the future, had forced the publisher to make the advance even more substantial and the scale of royalties even more generous.

The book had been published to catch the 1998 Christmas trade. As a familiar television face, Bill Stratton was wheeled out on all the daytime chat-shows, where he quoted a few 'by way of contrast' oddities, and smiled the self-depreciative crooked smile he had spent his entire career mastering.

The 'Christmas funny' market differs from many areas of the publishing business in that its books are never going to be read all the way through. Though it shares this quality with other categories — recipe books, gardening books and certain literary novels — nowhere else is the lack of ambition so blatant. The aim of a 'Christmas funny' is simply to ease the agony of an English Christmas Day afternoon. The food has been eaten, the presents distributed, the television listings ransacked in vain for anything watchable, and ill-matched family members are finally faced with the dreadful option of having to talk to each other. Old arguments about money seethe under the surface, resentments engendered in the nursery are about to be revived, criticisms based on changing attitudes to child-rearing are on the edge of being voiced. The forced bonhomie of the last few hours is about to implode.

Then, just before the fragile family shatters, someone picks up the 'Christmas funny' (a desperate gift to a relative without any discernible interests), flicks it open and lightens the threatening atmosphere by disclosing information about the size of the largest omelette ever made . . . or showing around the Japanese invention of a pocket-sized Jacuzzi . . . or pointing out hilarious photographs of dogs and cats with amusing speech bubbles. Compendiums of fart jokes are riffled through, politicians' gaffes ridiculed and, in that moment of family panic, even the collected works of humorous columnists become funny.

Hearty laughter follows. Over-hearty laughter, as the initial impact of the original joke gives way to the diminishing returns of repetition.

But the 'Christmas funny' has served its purpose. Staved off the renewal of family feuds. Bridged that ghastly half-hour gap until it is legitimate to say, 'Well, I think we probably ought to be off now.'

The 'Christmas funny' may be called upon to perform the same function a second time on Boxing Day, in those families unlucky enough to have two sets of ill-matched relatives to entertain. But, otherwise, it has achieved its end. Mission accomplished, the book can be relegated to a distant shelf or bedside table, never to be opened again — or to the loo, as an aid to concentration.

Because of people's desperation during the present-buying run-up to Christmas, the 'Christmas funny' market is now an over-crowded one. No idea is too silly, no celebrity too far down the alphabetical listings, for a tiny volume to be rushed out in the hopes of winning the publishing lottery, of becoming the 'Christmas funny' that gets into the bestseller lists.

Well, in 1998 Bill Stratton's *By Way of Contrast* was fortunate enough to achieve that envied status. He would never know to what degree the Christmas murder rate that year was reduced by tension-breaking readings about dysfunctional Welsh marriages, kittens trapped in handbags and the exploits of amorous snake-charmers.

All he did know was that the book sold and sold. Suddenly, through no effort of his own, Bill Stratton had become a bestselling author.

In 1999 and 2000 sequels followed. Rather imaginatively, they were called *By Way of Contrast 2* and *By Way of Contrast 3*. Though not selling as well as the original, they didn't do badly. And for each one, Sal Juster negotiated an even more substantial advance and an even more generous scale of royalty payments. Though his only creative input remained writing the two hundred and fifty word introduction (or, in fact, making minimal changes to the previous one), Bill Stratton's literary career blossomed.

The *By Way of Contrast* books generated a great deal of correspondence. Members of the public sent in their own news snippets of human foibles. When the books hit the bestseller lists, the flood of mail became so fierce that the publishers brought back a recently-retired office manager two days a week to deal with it. She was a woman of engaging cynicism called Carolyn, whose blondeness made no pretence at any origin other than a bottle. A well-rounded woman, spreading amiably towards fat, Carolyn had a taste for chunky gold jewellery, bright print dresses and cigarettes. Beneath the make-up her face had the egg-box quality of a heavy smoker, but nevertheless, she looked good. She possessed, in one of those withering phrases with which Andrea dismissed many women, 'an obvious sexuality'. (And whenever Andrea said that, the word 'brassy' lurked behind the phrase.)

Carolyn also possessed — more importantly for Bill Stratton — a son who was an expert in computers. Jason quickly set up a database for his mother to organise the *By Way of Contrast* clippings, and soon progressed to the creation of a *By Way of Contrast* website. He also originated the acronym BWOC for the company that developed.

Some contributions from the public were incorporated into the second two books, but the decision not to publish a fourth did not stop the flow of material. With the encouragement of Carolyn and Sal, Bill moved the operation away from the publishers. The investment was small, and Bill let himself be persuaded to set up the BWOC company out of curiosity more than anything else, just to see whether it took off. An office was rented just South of Vauxhall Bridge. Bill and his accountant were named as directors. Carolyn and Jason were the only staff. Jason was kept on a retainer as occasional consultant and computer fixer. Carolyn continued to go in two days a week at first, but soon there was enough business to occupy her for a full working week. Carolyn complained that she hadn't got to sixty simply to start work all over again, but she was very good at the job and, though she'd never give herself away by saying so, she clearly loved doing it.

Gradually, the BWOC operation grew. As well as mail from members of the British public, the website began to attract amusing trivia from all around the English-speaking world. Carolyn built up contacts with news agencies and local press reporters, and stories came from those sources too.

The thing that puzzled Bill Stratton about the whole operation was why — or, perhaps more accurately, how — it made money. He knew that the *By Way of Contrast* books still sold through the website, and he knew that Carolyn organised supplies of humorous snippets to after-dinner speakers, radio presenters and newspapers, but he still couldn't see that that was enough to bring in the profits it did. Carolyn and Jason had once tried to explain to him about the revenue from advertisers using the website and making links to other websites, but he didn't really understand.

Never mind. So long as the money rolled in, how it happened was really a detail. And all Bill Stratton had to do to receive his substantial cut of the profits was to attend the odd BWOC board meeting, make rare promotional appearances, and every week or so, drop in to show an interest in what Carolyn was doing.

He was scheduled for a visit to the Vauxhall office the day after he'd had dinner with Ginnie, and he felt blithe as he walked from Pimlico to the Vauxhall office. The Thames was in a sparkling tourist postcard mood, rather than its more usual slough of Dickensian murk. On that June day the city harmoniously blended the old and the new. Sunlight filtered out the fumes of pollution and despair.

And, as ever, the sun seemed to bring the breasts out. Bill knew that all women had breasts, all of the time. But some days they were a constant surprise to him. For months the existence of women's breasts was simply a fact of life, seen but not remarked upon, like telephone kiosks and zebra crossings. Then, suddenly one day they were everywhere. It was impossible to be unaware of them. They pressed against the webbing of haversacks, they jiggled on cyclists, they objected to the restraint of T-shirts.

Bill knew the phenomenon was partly an effect of the weather. The first really warm day of summer had rendered jackets redundant and brought out the breasts. Sleeveless tops emphasised that strange engineering of muscle between arms and breasts which was always so intriguing to men. Straps drew the focus tighter, and straps had proliferated since Bill Stratton's young day. For his mother a visible bra strap would have been as appalling a social gaffe as a shiny, unpowdered nose, but the girls he saw in the sun on Vauxhall Bridge seemed determined to show as many straps as possible, and in as many different colours (a lack of coordination which would again have appalled his mother).

He didn't know if it was Virginia Fairbrother's kiss of the night before which was setting him off, but Bill found himself, for the God-knew-how-many-millionth time, puzzling over the mechanics of lust. The breasts which had suddenly sprung up all around him were undoubtedly attractive, and undoubtedly made him think of sex. In an abstract way, he wanted to touch all of them, but he knew he couldn't — and indeed shouldn't. (He also knew, because he was well brought up, that he wouldn't.)

And if he did, he knew the contact would only lead to disillusionment. The chances of actually getting on with a woman whose breasts you wanted to touch in a public place were, he knew, infinitesimal. That perfect face and body glimpsed on the up escalator when you were going down was never, outside the world of romantic fiction, going to lead to the perfect relationship.

And yet the male lust reaction still responded every time, clicking into action like an automatic door everyone walks past but no one wants to go through. Breasts in public places are just a come-on, which every man knows will lead to disappointment, but which every man, like one of Pavlov's oldest and shaggiest dogs, still responds to.

By Bill Stratton's standards, that was quite a profound thought. But he didn't let it trouble him. Some days the prevalence of breasts could bring him down, make him reflect on his age, which was increasing, and his sexual experience, which hadn't increased for nearly forty years. But that morning, the breasts did not reproach him. They were just more of the beauties of London, sights to be seen. That morning nothing could shake Bill Stratton's mood. That morning Bill Stratton felt blithe.

Not only blithe, but positively virtuous. Approaching sixty, Bill had recently been summoned for a 'Well Man' MOT by his private health insurers, and the resulting report had been surprisingly positive. Yes, a few components were showing signs of wear, but no more than should be expected in a mechanism of that age. His teeth might need some attention before too long. He should probably drink less, and losing a little weight wouldn't hurt, but basically he was not a bad specimen of a male approaching his seventh decade.

He was also encouraged to take more exercise, hence the small glow of virtue he derived from walking the short distance over Vauxhall Bridge. Since his check-up, he used taxis a lot less for short journeys. Without going to the lengths of buying a bicycle, he walked a lot more and even paid a weekly visit to a gym. Bill was genetically fortunate in that he was never going to put on a lot of weight, but his new regime had reduced the incipient spare tyre around his waist. He was well aware — and if he hadn't been, Sal Juster's constant reminders would have made him aware — that a continuing supply of presentation work required him to take care of his appearance.

As ever, Carolyn had Radio Two and a cigarette on, and didn't hear Bill letting himself into the office. She was photocopying, with her back to him.

Again, it was probably his meeting with Ginnie the evening before that made him aware of what a particularly nice back Carolyn had. Like the breasts on Vauxhall Bridge, her curves were archetypally female, and Bill felt an urge he never had before; to place his hands on his employee's ample bottom.

Resisting was not difficult, but the fact that he had felt the temptation put him into a state of pleasant bewilderment. The confusions of the divorce had dammed up many of his feelings, and it was good to know they were beginning to trickle back.

Hopefully unaware of his thoughts, Carolyn became aware of his presence, and turned to face him. Her blue eyes held their usual scepticism, seeming to demand that everyone she met should prove themselves to her.

Bill found himself wondering whether she behaved the same in more intimate circumstances. Would a lover too have to face the hard challenge in those eyes? He racked his brains to remember the little he knew of

Carolyn's private life. The undeniable existence of Jason predicated the existence of a
father for him, but Bill didn't know whether
or not Carolyn had been married. He felt
pretty sure she was no longer married, if she
ever had been. Nor did he get the impression that she had a live-in partner. Perhaps,
in her sixties, she had given up all thoughts
of having a love life (which, given how nice
her back and her curves were, Bill thought
was a waste . . . for someone). All he knew
for certain was that Carolyn's generalised
cynicism became particularly intense when
she spoke of men.

'So . . . the big boss,' she said, as she
always did, her intonation at the same time
confirming that Bill was the big boss, and
subtly questioning his right to the role. Her
voice was unreconstructed South London.
The years she had spent in publishing had
not been allowed to sand down the rough-
ness of her origins, and the cigarettes she
had puffed throughout those years had ac-
centuated it. There was no 'side' to Carolyn. People took her as they found her, or
not at all. And it had to be said that,
throughout her career, people had been very
happy to take her as they found her.

'How's it going?' asked Bill, as he always
did.

She shrugged. 'The stuff comes in. People still want the stuff. What more can you ask?'

'Nothing.'

'Tea?'

He always said yes. The fact that he never drank tea outside the BWOC office was irrelevant. When Carolyn had first offered him tea, without the option of coffee, he'd accepted. And when she'd produced a cup that was heavily sugared, he had not demurred. Though sugar in any other form rarely passed his lips, it was part of his tea ritual with Carolyn, and he didn't dare to change any detail. He wasn't exactly frightened of her, but he could imagine the derision with which she would greet his announcement of what he really liked in the way of beverages. 'Oh, for God's sake, Bill, you idiot, why didn't you *say* . . . ?'

It was the same with the cigarettes. Neither Andrea nor he had ever smoked, although quite a lot of her NHS friends did. Without actually asking them to desist, Andrea had always made much of opening windows and fanning the air in the Putney kitchen. As a result, though Bill had echoed his wife's opinion whenever the subject came up, smoking held a guilty allure for him. Though he'd never take up the habit himself, he got a charge out of sharing Carolyn's cigarette-fuelled decadence.

The sweet hot tea tasted wonderful. Sweet hot tea is a traditional treatment for people in shock, and that morning Bill Stratton did feel as if he were in a state of shock . . . or at least in a state of comfortable confusion.

'Very good thing you and Andrea split up,' said Carolyn, typically direct.

'What?' asked Bill, who had not been expecting something quite so typically direct.

'I was amazed you stayed together so long. You never had anything in common.'

'I think we did.'

'Like what?' A characteristically confrontational challenge.

'Well . . . well. . . . We had the big house in Putney.'

Even as he said the words, Bill knew they weren't enough. But he was having great difficulty in coming up with any other answers to the question.

Carolyn snorted a reaction, but didn't pursue the subject. 'Anyway . . . how're you getting over the divorce?'

'Don't feel too bad.' Bill was relieved that the questions had got easier.

'No, well, it's all right for *men*. Always somehow come out of that kind of situation on top. Women need marriage — for many of them it's the only security they've got. But, come the break-up, it's men who always do best. Just one more of the advantages of being born with a tassel.'

Carolyn's views on the male of the species had nothing to do with feminism. In fact, they predated feminism by a long time. They reflected the accumulated observations of working class women over the centuries; that their menfolk were fundamentally lazy, and couldn't be trusted any further than you could see them.

Though he might have argued gender politics in more sophisticated company, Bill found Carolyn's attitude obscurely comforting. When a woman started from such a low base of expectation, there was much less chance of a man disappointing her. And men go through life in doom-laden fear of disappointing women.

'I like to think Andrea and I have achieved a civilised divorce.'

Carolyn blew out a derisive stream of smoke. 'No such thing. You'll both be seething vats of nit-picking resentments for the rest of your lives.'

'You may be right. But that's certainly not the way either of us is feeling at the moment.'

'How do you know what Andrea's feeling?'

'She's married to Dewi, who is apparently the great love of her life. She's able to be a Mother Hen to his children, which is apparently one of her lifetime ambitions. She has all the relationships she's ever wanted. I would imagine she's very happy.'

'And how about you?'

'What do you mean?'

'Have you got all the relationships you ever wanted?'

'I still don't understand.'

'I'm asking whether you've started on the geriatric dating trawl yet.'

'I think it's still a bit early after the break-up.'

'I thought you said that you were feeling fine.'

'Yes. But I want to get my breath. I don't want to rush into another long-term commitment.'

'I asked about dating, not long-term commitments. And I must say you're unusual even to mention the idea. Most men I've met wouldn't recognise a long-term commitment if it came up and slapped them in the face.' Carolyn's knee-jerk reaction had kicked in. The male gender could not be mentioned without a reference to its perfidy.

'I'm in no hurry.'

'Well, you should be. I know how old you are from the biog on the books. How long do you reckon you've got left?'

'I hadn't really thought about it.'

'Then you should have done. And don't just think about life expectancy, think in terms of *active* life. You should be cramming in as much activity as you can before everything drops off.'

'Is that what you're doing, Carolyn?'

Here was an opportunity to find out a little detail about her domestic circumstances, but the question was deflected by a brusque 'Chance'd be a fine thing.'

'I think your prognosis is a bit gloomy. You make it sound as if I'm in the Last Chance Saloon.'

'Damn nearly.'

Bill took a swallow of the wickedly sweet tea before redirecting the conversation. 'So . . . any good new ones?'

This was another part of their regular routine. To maintain the illusion that Bill had something useful to contribute to the running of BWOC, Carolyn would read out to him the pick of the latest *by way of contrast* stories. He loved the way she did this, totally flat, without a flicker of intonation, always reminding him of a woman in a joke

61

shop who'd once sold him 'one Comedy Nose, rubbery; one Tomahawk Through Head; one Dirty Dog Poo', without cracking a smile.

But he knew Carolyn's choice of delivery was deliberate. She didn't lack a sense of humour; her selection of the funniest items was unerring. She was just aware of the power of the deadpan.

'. . . and, "by way of contrast," ' she concluded, reading from the screen in front of her, ' "a man in Lytham St Anne's has perfected a method of speaking to gerbils, though he cannot yet understand what they're saying back to him." '

'Good,' said Bill. 'There seems to be no end to the supply.'

'The world's never going to run out of triviality — or people who prefer to hide behind it than face real life.' Carolyn kept coming up with remarks whose profundity was at odds with her blonde image. Beneath the deadpan surface, there was a lot more than met the eye.

'Presumably you'd like them printed up?' she went on, though the question did not need to be asked. Bill always wanted them printed up. His memory was still good, and he'd commit the latest list to heart. A new supply of funnies often proved useful at social occasions. Without waiting for his answer, Carolyn tucked a new cigarette into the corner of her mouth, clicked her mouse and the printer lurched into action. Its sound was large in the silence.

'Don't worry,' she said. 'Takes his time, but he'll come eventually.'

Bill instantly caught the reference. The printer did sound remarkably like an asthmatic approaching orgasm. He smiled and was rewarded by the flash of a knowing grin from Carolyn.

It was twelve-thirty when he said he ought to leave. For a moment, the unprecedented idea hovered in his mind of asking Carolyn to join him for a spot of lunch. But he didn't voice it.

Chapter four

. . . and, by way of contrast, a man in Cirencester, accused of disorderly behaviour after drinking two bottles of whisky, asked for another case to be taken into consideration.

'The trouble is,' said Trevor, 'that life's too bloody short . . .'

'Hm,' said Bill, neither supporting nor contesting the assertion.

'. . . and at the same time it's too bloody long. I mean, what we're all looking for is something that changes time . . . speeds it up, slows it down . . . though usually we want it speeded up . . .'

'Why?'

'Because otherwise it all takes too bloody long.'

'What takes too bloody long?'

'Life.'

'Ah.'

They were sitting in a pub in Bayswater, not far from Trevor's flat. In fact, very near Trevor's flat. The nearest pub, which Trevor regarded virtually as an annexe to the flat. In fact, he called it 'The Annexe'.

'Fancy meeting up for a drink in The Annexe?' was his customary summons, the one that got Bill there that evening.

They'd known each other for decades. Trevor had been an aspiring television news editor when Bill Stratton had started reading the bulletins. And they'd stayed friends, riding the rollercoaster of Trevor's professional and emotional life. Once, in a moment of sodden soppiness, he'd said, 'Wives may come and go, but a good friend like you, Bill mate, that's for ever.'

Trevor's most recent wife had been his fourth, but she'd left him, for much the same reasons as the first three. The BBC had indicated too that their relationship had had to end, but had at least left him with a pension which was sufficient for the maintenance of his small flat. And almost sufficient for the maintenance of its annexe.

Bill recognised the stage Trevor was at that evening. Stage Two. The effects of the lunchtime drinking had dissipated, leaving him low and self-hating. The first evening drink had diluted the gloom, creating a trance-like state in which he was prone to making remarks which sounded like profound gems of philosophy. Despite the portentousness of their delivery, all of these observations were complete cobblers. Later in the evening Trevor would become raucous and, at least in his own estimation, extraordinarily witty. Then, as his drinking companions drifted away, he would grow morose, and mourn his single state as, to his eyes, the nothing-to-write-home-about barmaid grew more and more beautiful.

Bill reconciled himself to hearing more pearls of philosophical wisdom, and sure enough they came.

'Thing is,' Trevor went on, 'life's a con-trick, really, but by the time you realise that, you're too caught up in the whole business to do much about it. And you're too old, too. By the time you realise what you should be doing, you've already done most of it.'

'Someone once said that experience is a comb that life gives you when you've lost your hair.'

'Well, he bloody hit the nail on the head, Bill, that bloke . . . whoever he was.' Trevor cast a mournful eye at his friend. 'Mind you, you're doing all right in that respect. You've still got some hair.'

'White, though.'

'If I'd got as much hair as you have, you wouldn't find me being picky about the colour. Anyway, if it bothers you, you could dye it.'

'It doesn't bother me that much. Anyway,

I don't want to go around with copper-beech-coloured hair.'

'Hmm?'

'That's what always happens. Think of the men you know who've got dyed hair. Why is that while women's hair colouring can range through every subtone of the natural palette — not to mention the unnatural one — men's dyed hair always ends up the colour of copper beech?'

'I don't know.' Trevor shook his head, apparently unwilling to pursue this interesting philosophical question. He took a long swallow from his pint, and looked dolefully around the bar. 'Alcohol speeds things up,' he said.

'Sorry? You've lost me.'

'What I was talking about earlier. We all need things that speed time up. Alcohol serves that purpose. Life's being a real drag, you can't believe how slowly the minute hand's moving . . . then you have a few drinks, and — bang — that's a whole evening disappeared. Five hours have gone without you noticing them.'

'Are you saying that's a good thing, Trevor?'

'Too bloody right I am. Think of the alternative.'

'Which is . . . ?'

'Every minute has taken a full bloody minute to go by. Sixty bloody seconds every time. Not even a fifty-nine second minute. You have to go the distance on every bloody one of them.'

'Why is that so terrible?'

'Because it's real. Full frontal reality. Not good for you. Humankind, it has been observed by one wiser than me, cannot bear very much reality. I know I can't.'

'But why not?'

'Because the real world is so bloody depressing.' Trevor raised his pint mug and peered through it. 'That's why I can only survive by looking through beer-tinted glasses.'

Early in every conversation with Trevor there came a reminder that he was a depressive. Bill, who'd never experienced the condition, could sympathise, but not empathise. And secretly he reckoned his friend got a lot of mileage out of his depression. The drinking was justified on the grounds that he was a depressive; so was his appalling lack of responsibility in the matter of women. No bad behaviour was the fault of Trevor Rainsford; it was always the fault of whatever malign deity had made Trevor Rainsford a depressive.

As ever, the mention of his depression

seemed to lift it a bit. He raised his glass again, this time to Bill. 'Congratulations.'

'On what?'

'On being unmarried.'

'I don't think I'm *un*married.'

'Then what are you?'

'Well . . .'

'Are you married?'

'No.'

'Then you're unmarried. By definition.'

This didn't seem right, but Bill couldn't fault the logic.

'And a good thing too,' Trevor went on.

'What is?'

'That you got away from Andrea.'

'But why?'

'Because you were so unsuited to each other. Everyone could see that.'

Everyone except me, thought Bill. He was getting a little miffed about the way everyone was getting at his marriage. Ginnie . . . Carolyn . . . now Trevor . . . not to mention Andrea herself. Was he the only person in the wide world who thought they'd had a vaguely workable marriage? Apparently so.

'Do you hear from her much?'

'No.'

'Lucky bastard. One or other of my ex-wives is on the phone every day, moaning about something. Usually money.'

'Andrea and I managed to sort out that side of things fairly amicably.'

'All right for some.'

'Do you still see any of them?'

'Not if I can help it.'

'See any of the children?'

'Not if they can help it.' Trevor let out a deep sigh. His lack of relationship with his children caused him a lot of depression . . . though not enough depression to make him go and try to build bridges with them. On the whole, he preferred the depression to the children.

'You were lucky not to have kids.'

'Yes.' Bill didn't want the conversation to proceed any further down that route. The discovery of Andrea's deliberate avoidance of conception was the area of his former marriage which continued to hurt most. 'You still betting on the horses?' he asked uncontroversially, knowing that the question would usually unleash a catalogue of equine disasters.

But to his surprise, Trevor answered, 'No. Given it up. What's the point? Either a horse is going to win or it isn't.'

'Come on, that's not the gambler's spirit.'

'True, though.'

'Yes, everyone knows it's true, but I thought gamblers were impervious to the

70

truth. Everyone knows betting's a mug's game, everyone knows that statistically you're almost definitely going to lose, but gamblers ignore that . . . keep their optimism in the face of the overwhelming justification for pessimism.'

'That's how gambling used to work with me, Bill, but, as with all illusions, once you've seen through it, you can never really believe again. It's like losing your faith.'

'And you've lost your faith in horses?'

'Totally. Gambling just doesn't do it any more. Which is a pity, because that's another of the activities that used to speed time up a bit for me. The tension of picking a horse to back, the build-up to the "off", the excitement of the race itself, the reaction to the result . . . even when it was a loss, which it usually was, half-hours could flash by during that process, until you were aware of time again. And then you could build yourself up again for the next race. . . . There was a stage when I'd bet on anything the betting shop would offer . . . horses, greyhounds . . . even virtual horse racing. I mean, how sad is that — grown men getting excited about contests between computer-generated animations of horses? But now . . .' Trevor shook his head mournfully.

'Doesn't do it for you?'

'Nothing does.' Another swig from the pint pot. 'Except this.'

'What about women? Now you too are *un*married?'

A lugubrious shake of the head. 'No more sex for me.'

'Why not?'

'Can't seem to do it. Bloody thing doesn't work any more.'

'Don't you think that might have something to do with the alcohol?'

'Who cares what it's to do with? All I know is that it's an unalloyed blessing. There was a period when even an undressed salad would get me randy, but that's all gone. When I think of all the time over the years I've wasted thinking about sex, trying to get sex, trying to get out of sexual relationships . . . you can't believe how good it is to know all that nonsense is over. I've even stopped having fantasies . . . God, the brain activity I used to devote to dreams of making it with a younger woman, you know, a pretty little thing in her twenties . . .'

For a moment the nostalgic thought almost rekindled something, but only for a moment. The fire was truly out. 'All gone, I'm glad to say.

'I mean, Bill, if you stop to think how much of a man's life is wasted by women.

Trying to get them into bed, yes, trying to get them to like you, but also — and this is the real time-waster — trying to understand them. That old Freud poser, "What do women want?" The answer is: nobody bloody knows. Even women don't know, so how the hell should poor pathetic men have an inkling? The point about the question is that, like all the really important questions of life, it doesn't have an answer. It's taken me far too long to realise that, but finally I have got a handle on it. And you can't believe the relief. I no longer feel guilty about my inability to understand women, because now I know for a fact that the assignment is impossible. For the first time in my life, I can think straight. My mind is completely unclouded.'

'So you cloud it up again with alcohol.'

'I know.' Trevor grinned. 'Bliss, isn't it?' He looked across at Bill, and once more raised his glass. 'Welcome to post-sex heaven.'

'I beg your pardon?'

'Count your blessings. You've managed to get out of your marriage to that witch Andrea . . . now you can enjoy yourself.'

'Yes, I intend to,' said Bill cautiously.

'And you never have to think about women again.'

73

The memories of Ginnie's kiss and Carolyn's back were too recent for Bill entirely to endorse that sentiment. He couldn't quite envisage a definition of 'enjoying himself' that involved no women at all.

'I think I'll let my mind follow its own course, Trevor. If it wants to stop thinking about sex, then fine. If not . . . well . . . I'll wait and see.'

'There is stuff you can take to stop you thinking about sex, you know . . .'

'What? Are you talking about bromide, given to the soldiers in the First World War — and supposedly during National Service too?'

'I'm not talking about bromide. I'm talking about *this*.' Trevor gathered up their glasses. 'Come on, we'll have a couple more of these.'

Chapter five

. . . and, by way of contrast, a man in New York has proposed to his psycho-therapist, reckoning marriage would be cheaper than paying her by the hour.

'You're still nursing a lot of anger.'

'I don't know that I am.'

'Believe me, Bill, you are. I've just read this book called *Anger: Men At Work*, and you fit perfectly into the B3 Category. You're a "Mr Nice Guy". You match the profile exactly.'

Bill offered no prompt, knowing that Sal would elucidate anyway. They were having lunch in a little Turkish place in Fitzrovia, just round the corner from the office of Sal Juster Associates. In so far as the vagaries of Sal's diets would allow, this was their most regular meeting place.

'It says in the book that "Mr Nice Guys" like to be liked.'

'Don't most of us?'

'Yes, but with them it's an obsession. And they're afraid that if they express anger, then people will stop liking them.'

'Sounds reasonable to me.'

'No, but the point is, they won't even express legitimate, justified anger. When someone's really shafted them, they'll still be nice to them.'

'Anything for a quiet life,' said Bill easily.

'It may be a quiet life, but it's not a healthy life. "Mr Nice Guys" are prone to stomach ulcers, sleep disturbance and depression.'

'Well then, I must be in the wrong category, because I don't suffer from any of those.'

'*Potentially*. You suffer from them *potentially*.'

'You mean they'll catch up with me one day?'

'Yes.'

'I can wait.'

'Bill, repressing anger is very dangerous. And you must have so much hatred of Andrea inside you that you're just not vocalising.'

'You don't know how much I vocalised it. When she first said she wanted a divorce, some fairly vicious comments were exchanged.'

'Yes, but that was just between each other. And now that you no longer have Andrea around to vocalise your anger to, you're suppressing it.'

'You're suggesting that I should moan on to everyone I meet about what a cow my ex-wife was?'

'Why not? That's what most divorcees do.'

'Well, I don't need to. Sorry to disappoint you, Sal, but I think I've pretty well got over the divorce.'

'Oh, you may think that, but you haven't. I read in this book, *The Relationship Amoeba: Splitting and Starting a New Life*, that to get over a divorce, it takes a month for each year that you were married.'

'Maybe I'm one of the lucky ones, who gets off more lightly than that.'

'I do worry about you, Bill.'

'That's very kind of you, and it's much appreciated. But it's not necessary.'

He grinned across at his agent. Sal Juster was small, with short dark hair, and rather endearingly stained teeth from the cigarettes she kept giving up and going back to again. Her navy-blue eyes were surrounded by wrinkles of permanent anxiety. She wasn't just anxious for herself, she was anxious for everyone else, and particularly for her clients. Her role in life was as a Little Miss Fixit. If she saw something was wrong with the circumstances of one of her friends, then her God-given mission was to sort it out. The trouble was that her friends were often totally unaware of the problems that she set out to fix for them.

Still, Bill appreciated her as a good agent and a pleasant lunch companion. She didn't look as old as the sixty years which mere mathematics dictated she must have lived. And she never talked of retirement; 'Agents don't retire,' she said. Her make-up was heavy, with punctiliously defined lips and eyebrows. She was full-breasted, and would probably have been plumper but for the ever-changing regimes of dieting and exercise to which she subjected her body.

Her emotional life had been chequered — indeed positively tartan — and she changed partners as frequently as she changed belief systems. Given her history of relationship disasters, she remained surprisingly optimistic. Just as she continuously believed she would one day find the perfect lifestyle, so she was certain she would eventually find the perfect man (or woman — she'd tried both).

In spite of her moments of sheer loopiness, Bill liked Sal, and in his newly-awoken state, found himself wondering what it would be like to go to bed with her. Interesting, certainly — he felt sure she'd put as much research into sexual technique as she had to all other aspects of her life. No, the sex would be fun. What might not be quite so much fun would be the inevitable deconstruction of the act afterwards. And the quotations from all the books she would have read on the subject.

'I still don't believe you,' Sal went on. 'You must be bottling up a lot of resentment.'

'Why?'

'All those years with Andrea. "The corrosion of continuity." '

'I beg your pardon?'

'It's a quotation from a book called *Throttling the Individual: An Analysis of Marriage*. It says how destructive living with someone totally unsuitable for you can be.'

'You're saying Andrea was totally unsuitable for me?'

'Always. Totally.'

Another to add to the list of gloomy commentators on his marriage. If they all thought that, why had none of them said anything before? He suspected there might be an element of hindsight here. He knew the divorce had polarised his and Andrea's friends. Those who had decided to join his faction perhaps felt they needed to be extravagantly anti-her. And possibly, gathered round a sizzling nut cutlet in the Roberts household in Muswell Hill, Andrea and Dewi's friends were equally dismissive of Bill Stratton.

'Yes, well, if you don't mind, Sal, I'd quite like to move off the subject of my marriage. When I arrived here today, I was feeling quite good about it, had come to terms with the situation, but now —'

'Ah, no, you only *think* you've come to terms with the situation. There's a very good bit on that in this book *Front-Loading: The Masks We Make for* —'

He raised both hands in supplication. 'Please. Could we just talk about anything other than my marriage?'

'Like what?'

'Well, why not my so-called "career"? You are my agent, after all.'

'Yes . . .' Sal hesitated for a moment, unwilling to give up the opportunity of sorting out Bill's post-divorce trauma, but decided she could always come back to that. 'All right, I did want to talk to you about work, anyway. I think the moment has come for us to get pro-active.'

'Oh?'

'Now you no longer have Andrea holding you back, it's time for us to maximise your earning potential.'

'Just a minute. I wasn't aware that Andrea

ever "held me back".'

'Of course she did. She disapproved of you capitalising on your commercial appeal.'

'She never said that.'

'She didn't have to say anything. She'd just wrinkle her nose at the idea of you being paid for opening supermarkets or handing out prizes at awards ceremonies.'

When he thought about it, Bill realised that Sal was probably right. Andrea had always been dismissive of celebrities 'prostituting themselves', and she had been pretty sniffy about the personal appearances — or 'PAs', as they were known in the business — that he had done. The further he got away from the marriage, the more he could sympathise with the outsiders' views of it. Andrea and he really had had very little in common.

'She thought that stuff was beneath you, Bill.'

'Maybe.'

'But you don't, do you?'

'God, no. I might question the sanity of someone who'd be prepared to pay me for doing that kind of stuff, but I have no reservations about doing it.'

'Good. I'll do some ringing round. Lots of people always looking for PAs — any name from the television, doesn't matter who it is.' Bill had known this reality for so long that it had no power to wound him. 'And I really do think it's time you were launched on the after-dinner speaking circuit. You always used to say your evenings were sacrosanct, you liked spending them with Andrea . . .'

'Yes.'

'Though from various other things you said, I gather she was out most evenings doing health service committee work and what-have-you . . .'

Once again, Sal had come very close to the truth. There had certainly been more busy evenings for Andrea towards the end of the marriage. Idly, Bill wondered whether they had been genuine health service committees, or 'what-have-you' cover-ups for evenings spent with Dewi. Presumably the affair had started with clandestine, snatched moments and paroxysms of guilt. Bill wondered how much the knowledge would have worried him if he'd been aware at the time. It certainly didn't worry him now. He seemed to be coming round to the consensus view, that the only thing remarkable about his marriage was that it had lasted as long as it did.

'Anyway, now you don't have that

problem, I can really start building up the after-dinner bookings for you.'

'Whoa, whoa, Sal, just a minute. One thing you're forgetting is that I've never done an after-dinner speech in my life.'

'Not technically, but for heaven's sake, you've spent your entire professional life talking in public.'

'*Reading* in public. Big difference.'

'No, it's not. For an after-dinner speech, you just learn what you would otherwise have read. Easy-peasy.'

'But people who do after-dinner speaking are usually people who've done something with their lives. So they have something to talk about.'

'A lot of them have never done anything. They're just people who the audience recognises from the television, who stand up, drop a few names, and tell a few jokes. You fit the profile perfectly.'

'Thank you. I would point out, though, that I don't know any jokes.'

'Bill, you have the biggest archive of jokes of anyone I know.'

'How do you mean?'

'Are you being deliberately dense? BWOC.'

'Oh.'

'What is BWOC but an infinite resource of funny stories?'

'I suppose you're right. I'd never thought of using it in that way.'

'Really, Bill. You have the commercial instinct of a frozen pea. Of course you can use it. All tried and tested lines —'

'And all — however unlikely they sound — genuine news stories.'

'Exactly. They're perfect. Combining humour and journalistic integrity — what a formula. They'd go down a storm on the after-dinner circuit. And also, the great thing is, that's what the audience expects of you. They see your name and they immediately think "by way of contrast". The fact that you then tell a stream of "by way of contrast" stories is exactly what they want from you.'

'Hmm . . .' He was rather coming round to the idea.

'Tell you what. I'll make one booking for you some time in the next few weeks, just as a try-out. You knock together twenty minutes of BWOC stories — or get Carolyn to do it for you — and we'll give it a go.'

'Well . . .'

'If you're really scared, I'll come and hold your hand for the first one.'

'I might be glad of that. By the way, Sal, can I ask . . . what sort of money would we be talking for doing this stuff?'

She told him. It seemed a ridiculously large amount. 'But then of course, as you get better known, we can ask for quite a lot more.'

The waitress offered him more chili sauce on his Iskender Kebab, and he accepted. But it wasn't the spiciness that brought a glitter to Bill Stratton's eye. It was the feeling of a new life — or perhaps a whole number of new lives opening up in front of him.

'Ooh, another thing, Bill . . .'

'Mmm?'

'Could you come to dinner on Saturday?'

'Dinner? Where?'

'My place.'

Though he'd know Sal for more than ten years, they'd always met at lunchtimes, in the anonymity of restaurants. To be invited to his agent's home for an evening was another new departure.

Sal seemed to read his thoughts. 'I never invited you before, because of Andrea.'

'What was so wrong with Andrea?' But it was a token protest; rather than leaping, he was shuffling to his ex-wife's defence.

'You *know*. She was just so worthy. She'd make me and my friends feel unworthy about being obsessed by the media. She'd make us all feel guilty.'

Bill pondered this. Maybe that was what Andrea had done all through their marriage, made him feel guilty. . . . Made him feel guilty for what, though? Back to his being shallow, he supposed. He hadn't been aware of feeling guilty during the marriage, but distance was certainly giving him a new perspective.

He also began to wonder why Sal had issued this sudden invitation. Had she interests in him beyond the purely professional? Had she found some book in the 'Mind, Body and Spirit' section about mixing business with pleasure?

But the notion was dispelled by her next words. 'It's a dinner party I'm giving on Saturday night. Got odd numbers.'

'And I can even them up?'

'Yes,' she replied with disarming frankness. 'You see, Bill, you have now become something even more useful than a Swiss Army Knife.'

'A spare man?'

'Exactly.' She smiled smugly at him. 'I'm going to use you shamelessly.'

'Oh.'

'Dinner parties, meals out, theatre, cinema . . . you can be my tame companion.'

'How do you know I'd be tame?'

'Because I know you, Bill.'

Fair enough. She was probably right.

'You can be my front.'

'Front for what?'

'Front to stop people asking me if I'm in a relationship or not.'

'And are you in a relationship? Or not?'

The wrinkles between the navy-blue eyes deepened at the difficulty of the question. 'Oh, these things are so difficult to be specific about, Bill. There's a very good chapter on "The Definition of Twoness" in a book called *What We Mean When We Say What We Mean . . .*'

And so the lunch continued.

Chapter six

. . . and, by way of contrast, a match-maker in New York gave up the business after one of his clients went off with his wife.

Sal Juster's flat was in a mansion block in Maida Vale, a surprisingly spacious set of interconnecting rooms that seemed to go on for ever. Because he was making his first visit there, Bill Stratton was unaware how frequently the positioning of the flat's furniture was changed, according to Sal's latest readings of *feng shui* or other lifestyle advocacies.

What he saw, however, looked very opulent. He didn't flatter himself that Sal could afford such luxury on fifteen per cent of his earnings, but he knew she had many other higher profile, and therefore more lucrative, clients.

To his surprise, he'd felt quite nervous at the prospect of the evening, marking as it did a change from the purely professional relationship he'd hitherto enjoyed with Sal. Though not an excessive drinker, he had fortified himself with a couple of large scotches in Pimlico, and Sal's introductions over welcoming champagne went by in something of a haze.

There were three couples there. Two were married, but even the unmarried set carried that unmistakable air of coupledom about them. One pairing was clearly second time around for the man. The wife had to be twenty years younger, and there was much talk of children. In the husband's old eyes, pride in his trophy wife had long since given way to sheer horror at the thought of going through small children and school fees again.

To Bill's surprise, there was also a guest who had a distinctly proprietorial attitude to Sal. Had he not announced the fact to everyone, his grey straggling ponytail would have proclaimed him to be something in the music business. He spoke dated black slang in an accent from which he had not totally managed to eradicate his public school education. He announced that he was called Eli, but the challenging way he did so suggested that it probably wasn't the name he had been christened with. From what was said during the evening, his relationship with Sal was relatively new. And, Bill suspected, unlikely to get very old.

Then there was Maria. Though normally

good with names, the Scotch or his nervous-
ness made it hard for Bill to fix the identities
of the other guests. He remembered all the
names he'd been given on introduction, but
he couldn't be precise about which was attached to which guest. With Maria, though,
he had no problems.

She was a short — what his mother would
have called 'petite' — woman with sparkling
brown eyes in a face Oil-of-Olayed into a
fine sheen and then cunningly touched with
make-up. Her skin was tanned from a
recent visit to somewhere more exotic than
the British Isles, but was taut, without that
crumpled look sun-browning can give to an
older woman. Her body was thin, but her
breasts full, with an endearing crinkle of
flesh between them. She wore a light silk
print dress and high heels which flattered
her slender legs. There was a lot of gold
jewellery, which didn't include a wedding
ring.

She had worked in PR — or maybe still
did work in PR. Bill hadn't quite got that
clear. Maybe he hadn't been concentrating,
or maybe Maria had deliberately left such
details obscure.

Obviously she recognised him as Bill
Stratton from the television. Everyone over
a certain age did. And within minutes of

meeting, she had mentioned his 'by way of contrast' catchphrase. Again, everyone over a certain age did.

This prompted him to tell her a few choice gems from the BWOC collection. They were mostly lines he had trotted out on chat-shows when promoting the books, but he was surprised how well he remembered them. Maybe Sal's idea of his converting them into after-dinner speaking material wasn't so daft after all.

Maria didn't seem to know the other guests very well, though she had the social skills demanded by her profession, and could clearly maintain a conversation with anyone about anything. But in fact she spent most of the pre-dinner drinks being amused by Bill. And when it came to eating, the serendipity of the seating plan also put him next to her. As he drank more and presented his BWOC lines to a more general audience, he was aware of showing off for Maria's benefit, of gauging her reactions, and feeling gratified when he gained a big laugh from the assembled throng.

The insistent feeling came to Bill that perhaps life with Andrea had suppressed his social skills. Her circle of friends never wanted to hear anything funny and, since all he knew of NHS iniquities was what Andrea had told him, he rarely had much to contribute to their conversation. Whereas at Sal Juster's dinner party, the consensus seemed to be that Bill Stratton was rather a witty fellow.

Maria certainly seemed to appreciate his company.

Bill couldn't believe how quickly the evening passed — he seemed only just to have arrived when the young wife and her haunted husband began murmuring about babysitters and leaving. Then the other guests started looking at their watches too.

Nor could Bill believe how smoothly things were going between him and Maria. When it came to Sal calling cabs, geographical logic dictated that, since they were both going South, Bill and Maria should share one down as far as her flat near Marble Arch, from whence he would continue to Pimlico. But then, when they arrived outside her block and she suggested his coming in 'for a final drink', continuing to Pimlico didn't seem so important. Any disquiet the cabbie might have felt about the shortened trip was dissipated by an absurdly generous tip (although that still didn't wipe the smug, knowing smile off his face).

Bill didn't care, anyway. In the lift Maria seemed to stumble against him, and it made sense to put his hands on her shoulders to steady her. Then her fragrant hair seemed very close to his face, and giving her a gentle kiss on the forehead was entirely natural. When her face turned up to his, their lips automatically engaged.

The interior of Maria's flat had recently been done by a very exclusive designer, but Bill didn't take in much of the makeover. The minute they were inside the door, Maria's mouth and his re-engaged, their hands started to scrabble at the frontiers of cloth and flesh, and all he was really aware of was overpowering lust.

He tried to remember when he'd last felt lust on that scale. The routine of sex with Andrea had regulated his passion to a kind of twice-a-week supply-and-demand basis. When she showed reluctance to continue, he had reconciled himself to the ending of that particular phase of his life. And though, like most men, he could still be suddenly inflamed by a cleavage on a poster or a flash of thigh on the tube, most of the time his lust was subdued into a kind of half-life. Lacking the expectation of fulfilment, his sex-drive had gone into neutral.

But touching Maria had brought it back to life in turbo-charged splendour. The fact that everything still appeared to work made him feel wonderful. Or he would have felt wonderful were it not for the sensation of intense urgency.

She separated herself far enough away from him to ask, 'Shall I get that drink?'

'Do you think we'll need it?'

'Be as well.' And she'd slipped out of his grasp into the kitchen. Bill stood disconnected. For a moment he contemplated sitting down, but decided it would be too painful.

She appeared from the kitchen with an open bottle of champagne and two glasses. With a knowing wink, she led the way to her bedroom.

After hurried gulps of champagne, they entangled together on the bed. Fingers scrabbled, poppers popped, zips unzipped, inhibitions melted in a silkiness of underwear.

Fortunately alcohol worked its timeless magic, and Bill was naked and in bed with Maria before he'd time to worry about the white hairs on his chest, or his pale incipient paunch, or the purple threads of veins around his ankles. And the immediacy of lust made him equally blind to any imperfections of her body (assuming, which a gentleman wouldn't, that there were any).

But, to his surprise, moments before they

conjoined, he found himself asking, 'Should we?'

'What do you mean — "should we"?'

'Well, just . . .' He couldn't come up with a satisfactory verbal answer, but he seemed to be coming up with an unarguable physical one, and the 'should' question became irrelevant.

After nearly forty years of Andrea's, another body was strange. Maria's mouth tasted different, felt different, was at a different angle. The outline of her bottom was different, the contour of her breasts different. Everything was different.

Different, but by no means unappealing.

Bill Stratton was making love to another woman. And it all seemed to be going rather well.

Or so Maria, through her moans, asserted. Bill had never really known whether or not he was a good lover. Inside a marriage like his, such a question had not arisen. Neither he nor Andrea had much grounds for comparison. And when she had had grounds for comparison — in other words, Dewi — she had given the impression there *was* no comparison. Dewi was 'what she'd been looking for all her life'; he made her 'feel like a woman'. So Bill, having failed for so long to give Andrea either of these satisfactions, concluded that he probably wasn't a very good lover.

But that was not the message he was getting from Maria. Even through the distractions of what his body was feeling, his mind was sufficiently detached to know that her commendation might be part of a routine. Flattery, women's magazines insisted, was a necessary stimulus to the male libido. But Maria did sound as though she meant what she was saying.

And Bill began to wonder whether, in fact, Andrea hadn't taught him rather well. She had certainly known what she wanted in bed, and guided him to the actions that gave her pleasure. These involved the use of hands, lips and tongue at least as much as any other part of his anatomy. And Maria seemed to appreciate such ministrations too.

Also, though it was only during the very earliest moments of his married life that Bill had suffered from premature ejaculation, it had to be said that, with the years, his ejaculation had become increasingly mature. And Maria seemed to appreciate that slowness too.

At the moment when he finally came, he saw over her shoulder on the bedside table a framed photograph. Taken fairly recently from the way she looked. In a garden, with a woman who had to be her daughter, and a young man who logic dictated was her son-in-law. And four small children. Undoubtedly four grandchildren.

But, in the haze of Maria's carefully-lit bedroom, he didn't feel as though he were cuddling a grandmother. Or, to put it another way, cuddling a grandmother didn't seem like such a bad idea. Even though, after his orgasm, he became more aware of the difference of her body from Andrea's, the different way her flesh was distributed, the different areas of hardness and softness.

Gallantly, he disentangled himself from her only to pour them more champagne, which they drank before returning to their cuddle. They didn't say much. There didn't seem much to say. But the silence between them was benign.

They must have dozed. Bill woke blearily to a totally unprecedented sensation — Maria's hand working with some determination between his legs.

'Come on,' she murmured throatily, 'I'm sure there's a little more where that came from.'

This was uncharted territory for Bill. Uncharted since the very early days of his marriage, when a certain rampancy had ruled.

At least thirty years must have passed since he last came twice in the same session.

Marital sex tends to stop after the orgasm. Certainly after the male orgasm (though hopefully the woman has got something out of it too). A little friendly kiss perhaps, then roll apart to continue worrying about the mortgage.

With Maria, though, he didn't even know if she had a mortgage. But he sure as hell knew that he didn't have a joint one with her. Which was very comforting. As his body came reassuringly back to life, Bill realised that he knew almost nothing about Maria. Their dinner table conversation hadn't been very revelatory. All he knew about her was that she was manipulating his body with a great deal more enthusiasm than Andrea had ever shown. He let himself go with the flow — or at least go till the flow.

And the second flow was even more enjoyable than the first. But again, once the expressions of flattery and gratitude had been made, there didn't seem a lot to say.

The remains of the champagne were consumed.

And eventually, Bill Stratton said the inevitable. 'Well, I suppose I'd better be on my way.'

He wasn't sure how this was going to be

taken. Maria knew he was divorced, so wouldn't be assuming he had a wife to get back to. Equally, he didn't feel up to the effort of inventing reasons why he had to get back to Pimlico — fictional dogs to walk, dependent aged relatives, demands of an early start in the morning.

But Maria took it like a lamb. 'Yes. All been very nice, but we don't want the magic to fade, do we?'

'Well, if you want me to stay . . .' he began, not sure how he could end the sentence.

Fortunately she didn't give him time to. 'No, that's fine. Keep your illusions. I don't look so good in daylight.'

'Nor me,' he chuckled, as he eased his body off the bed. He did now feel very tired. And the accumulated alcohol was getting to him, as well.

He also felt awkward. No one looks good getting dressed, and he didn't know whether to reassume his scattered clothes facing Maria or with his back to her. Facing, she'd see his white chest hair and incipient paunch. Turned away, she'd see his rather creased bottom and the little knot of bluish veins behind his right knee.

Instinctively, Maria seemed to sense his dilemma. Lifting herself up off the bed, she moved towards the bathroom door. 'Going to run myself a bath. Don't know if you fancy one? Or a shower?' She didn't make the invitation over-pressing.

'No, I'll do that at home. Maybe just a quick wash.'

She drew aside to let him into the bathroom. He washed a small part of him (a very small part by now). Then they changed rooms and he dressed in private.

When he was ready he knocked on the bathroom door. Maria opened it, revealing herself dressed in a fluffy dressing gown. She had started to take off her make-up. Her brown eyes were deeper set in wrinkles. There were slight lines of puckering around her mouth, and when she smiled, he could see the skilled bridgework of her teeth.

'Just wanted to say thank you for having me,' said Bill fatuously.

'The pleasure was all mine.'

'I can assure you it wasn't.'

'Good. Can you let yourself out? Just make sure the door clicks shut after you.'

'Of course.'

'Goodbye.'

She puckered her lips further. He gave them a dry kiss.

'Be in touch.'

'Yes.'

It was nearly half-past three. He found a

roaming late-night cab with a mercifully taciturn driver, whose silence was rewarded with a large tip when he drew up outside the Pimlico flat.

And, as Bill Stratton entered his domain, he felt really good. He had a sex life again.

Even ignoring the dubious qualification claims of his pre-Andrea fumble, his personal total was now undeniably two. He knew there were people who had achieved that milestone before they were sixty, but that didn't take away from his achievement.

His other response was entirely masculine. At the welcome moment of the first climax with Maria, he hadn't thought, 'I look forward to doing this many more times with this woman.' He had thought, 'I look forward to doing this many more times with lots of other women.'

Chapter seven

. . . and, by way of contrast, a local authority initiative to cut down gossip in a Gloucestershire village failed because everyone knew about it three weeks before it was launched.

'So?' asked Sal on the phone at eleven o'clock the following morning.

'So what?'

'You and Maria.'

'What about me and Maria?'

'Come on. You went off together.'

'We shared a taxi, because we were both going south.'

'Yes, yes, yes. But you spent the entire evening gobbling each other up with your eyes.'

'So?'

'I want to know how far the gobbling continued.'

Bill felt rather shaken by this interrogation. He'd woken only half an hour before, tired but surprisingly not hungover. His head felt light and scoured, but his mind felt good. The events of the previous night had left him with a warm, almost complacent, glow.

And, for a while, he wanted to enjoy that glow. He certainly didn't want to analyse its causes.

Sal, though, evidently did. 'Come on, tell me.'

He played for time. 'Oh, I did want to say thank you for the evening. Lovely dinner. I was going to ring you, but —'

'Never mind that. I want to know what happened last night.'

'What makes you think anything happened last night?'

'Call it women's intuition. Or in fact don't bother with women's intuition. Maria told me she fancied you.'

'Oh? When?'

'When she nipped out to the kitchen, ostensibly to help me with the coffee. She'd really come out to thank me.'

'Thank you for what — the dinner?'

'No, you fool. To thank me for setting it up.'

'Setting what up?'

'God, you're being obtuse, Bill. To thank me for setting up you and her.'

'You mean it was a set-up?'

'Of course it was. I'm not an agent for nothing, you know. And being a hostess is very much the same job. You find the right people, you put them in touch, you hope something will come of it.'

'Ah.'

'Stop sounding so innocent, Bill. Surely you could see what was happening? Maria was the only single woman there, you were the only single man.'

'What about Eli? He's a single man.'

'Last night Eli was with me. Though,' Sal continued with an edge of steel in her voice, 'this morning he's about to become single again.'

'Oh, what, are you going to tell him to —'

'Don't change the subject, Bill. We're not talking about me and Eli. We're talking about you and Maria. Come on, give me the dirt.'

Bill was in a state of bewilderment. Obviously he was aware that matchmaking happened. During their marriage Andrea had occasionally set up dinner parties where some sad bereaved anaesthetist was meant to get off with a recently-dumped nurse. But Bill hadn't anticipated finding himself in that situation. The divorce must have affected him more than he realised. Preoccupations with its details had fuddled his thinking, slowed down his reflexes, allayed his suspicions.

So . . . he and Maria had been set up. Obvious, now he came to think about it. Why had he been so innocent the night before?

He tried to work out whether this new knowledge changed his reactions to the previous night's events. What had felt totally spontaneous now seemed, in retrospect, a little calculated. But that didn't worry him too much. More disturbing was the fact that what he'd thought of as a private encounter now had a public dimension. Sal knew all about it. And if Sal knew, a lot of other people would also soon know.

But was that such a bad thing? He wasn't betraying anyone. Given the difference in their social circles, news of his assignation with Maria was very unlikely to have reached Andrea, but if it did, so what? Could be rather a good thing, actually, demonstrating that he wasn't moping for her, wasn't envying her domestic cosiness with Dewi, was in fact getting on with his own life.

He'd still rather Sal didn't know about it, though.

But undeniably she did. And, what's more, she wanted every last gory detail.

'Give me the dirt,' she repeated.

'I don't think,' Bill replied, in a voice of aristocratic decorum, 'that it is proper for a gentleman to reveal the secrets of a lady's boudoir.'

'Well, if you don't tell me, I'll find out from Maria.'

'Maybe she too,' said Bill, maintaining his formal manner, 'has some instinct for discretion, and will not respond to your vulgar interrogation.'

'Don't you believe it, sunshine. Been such a long time waiting that, now Maria's finally got laid, everyone in London will know about it within twenty-four hours.'

This was another ramification of his actions that Bill had not anticipated. Indeed, the more he thought about his situation, the more he realised how little he had anticipated of anything. He wondered what the chances were of anyone he knew hearing about his amorous adventure. How different from his own were Maria's social circles? He realised he hadn't a clue. Except that she worked — or had worked — in PR, and that she was a grandmother, he knew absolutely nothing about his previous night's sexual partner.

With slight shock at his own callousness, he recognised that he wasn't that interested in finding out more about her either.

'Well, if you're going to be a spoilsport and clam up on me,' said Sal, affecting the tone of an aggrieved child, 'I'll just have to get the dirt from Maria herself. Have you rung her yet?'

Bill was puzzled. 'No. Why should I?'

'For heaven's sake, Bill! You have been out of the dating loop for a long time, haven't you?'

'I've been married to Andrea for most of the last forty years.'

'Yes, of course. You poor bugger. Sorry, allowances must be made. The thing is . . .' her voice took on a school-teacherly quality '. . . even though there is now more equality between the genders, even though men and women act as free sexual agents, a woman who invites a man into her bed *does still appreciate the courtesy of a thank you call the next day!*'

Her final screech was so strong he had to move the phone away from his ear. 'Yes, of course, Sal. Of course I'm going to be in touch with Maria. Give me a chance, though. I've only just woken up.'

'All right.' His words had calmed her. 'Just make sure you don't forget.'

'I won't.'

'Good. Meanwhile,' Sal continued gleefully, 'I'll get on to her, and find out your marks out of ten . . . not to mention bonuses for artistic impression. I'll phone her straight away.' Doubt crept into her voice.

'Or maybe I should dump Eli first, then call Maria . . . ?'

'I can't possibly advise you on that.'

'I think dump Eli first. I can't really tell Maria what crap he was in bed while he's still here.'

Another shadow flickered across Bill's sunny disposition. Was Maria about to give Sal a blow-by-blow (damn, they hadn't got round to doing that) account of *his* sexual prowess?

'Well, sorry it didn't work out with you and Eli,' he said formally.

'Never had a chance. You see, I'm a Virgo and Eli's Sagittarius. I should have remembered what I read in that book *Astroturf-out: How To Dump Incompatible Lovers*. With the configurations of stars at Eli's birth, there was no chance that we were going to have a physical conjunction that was anything but . . .'

Bill Stratton was thoughtful as he set his coffeemaker to produce some really brain-kicking espresso. The phrase 'whole new ball-game' kept rising to his mind. Dear, oh dear, had he somehow managed to enter the murky world defined by the awful word 'dating'?

He'd had a really enjoyable — and very

necessary — sexual encounter with Maria. And he wouldn't mind, at some point, having the same again. The one thing he didn't want to have with her was . . . he felt another awful word creeping into his mind . . . a 'relationship'.

He knew that was a very masculine response, but, for God's sake, he was a man. What else did anyone expect from him?

And yet. . . . And yet. . . . He didn't want to be thought a heel. The pathetic desire to be liked had been the guiding principle of his life. For most of his marriage, that hadn't been a problem. He had believed that Andrea liked him (though that may have been an illusion), and her earnest friends at least tolerated him as her trivial appendage. But now . . . he needed someone to explain the rules of the complex new world in which he found himself.

The espresso was ready. He took perverse pleasure in scalding his mouth as his system took in its first caffeine shock.

Sal had been right. He did need to contact Maria. Not to do so would be simply churlish. He stretched out his hand towards the phone.

But immediately doubt assailed him. What should he say to her? He trusted himself to come up with something more gracious than a 'Thank you, ma'am' to follow his 'Wham' and his 'Bam', but exactly what would be appropriate to his new circumstances? He tried to remember their conversation of the night before, but all that came back to him were BWOC lines. Maybe that was all their conversation had consisted of.

No, tricky to talk to her. He might end up revealing too much about himself, or taking on the role of porter for her baggage. There had to be a safer way. He reached for the *Yellow Pages*.

Surprising how many florists there were in Central London. He supposed they'd always been there, but when you're not looking for something, you don't see it. Surprising also, for a rare user of the service, how many of them offered same day delivery 'at no extra cost'.

He dialled the first number on the list, and the transaction was quickly concluded. Rejecting red roses as hazardously symbolic, he settled on a Large Hand-Tied Display of Summer Blooms. He decided against adding Belgian Chocolates or a Bottle of Champagne.

Yes, that would do. A gentlemanly gesture. A holding operation.

While the details of his order were being

checked, he decided how he'd spend the rest of his day. There was a local pub near the Thames, where he had enough acquaintances to ensure a pleasant boozy lunchtime. Then he'd catch up on some of the previous night's sleep.

When the patient florist at the other end of the line asked what message he wanted to send with the flowers, Bill came up with: '. . . and, by way of contrast, thank you for an unforgettable experience.'

Then he went down to the pub to try and forget about it.

It was about six when the phone rang. He felt better after a couple of hours sleep and had recovered from the bleariness of waking. A contentment about the events of the previous night had returned.

'It's Ginnie.'

'Oh, hello.' Good heavens, did she know about Maria too? But the anxiety was quickly defused. The actress had never met Sal, she moved in completely different social circles. He was being paranoid.

'I'm ringing because I find myself at a loose end this evening.'

'Oh?'

'I was meant to be taking part in a programme of readings in support of a

111

writer who's imprisoned in China, but it's been cancelled.'

'Why?'

'Chinese authorities released him on Thursday.'

'Oh.'

'No sense of theatre, these totalitarian regimes. We've had to pull the plug on the whole show.'

'Bad luck.'

'I'll survive. So, anyway, I find myself with this lovely, juicy Sunday evening free. And, since there's never anything to watch on television on Sunday evening . . .'

This was absolutely true, but Bill had still intended to watch it. That's what he felt like, a little undemanding cosseting. Mindless television and a few glasses of wine would do the trick.

'So, anyway,' Ginnie went on, 'I'm at a loose end . . . and if you happened to be at a loose end too . . . well, I thought we could meet up for a bit of supper . . . ?'

'I'd love to, but I'm afraid I'm committed elsewhere.'

Bill was surprised by the speed and the instinctiveness of the lie. Also by why he'd lied. An evening with Ginnie had got to be more interesting than Sunday night television schmaltz.

'Oh.' She was too professional to sound put down. 'Don't worry. Very short notice, just the off-chance. We must do it another time.'

'I'd love that.'

'Give me a call.'

'Oh, I will, Ginnie. Of course I will.'

After he'd put the phone down, he found himself still in a state of mild shock at his behaviour. Ginnie meant far more to him than the woman he'd been with the previous night, and yet he'd instinctively turned down the offer of her company. Surely he hadn't done it for reasons of guilt?

No, he didn't feel guilty. Maybe he feared that, caught in the beam of Ginnie's perceptive hazel eyes, he wouldn't be able to keep his encounter with Maria a secret. But why would it matter if he did own up to what he'd done? He wasn't betraying anyone. He had no one to betray.

It was still the speed of his knee-jerk instinct to lie that surprised him. Maybe, now he had entered into the world of different women, surreptitiousness had become essential. There was no necessity for everyone to know everything. Kissing and telling was a course which held no attraction for Bill Stratton. He would become more cautious, secretive even, controlling the flow of information that he vouchsafed to his various friends.

Ten minutes after he had put the phone down, the thought of seeing Ginnie that evening had become more attractive. He contemplated ringing her back, telling her he'd managed to untangle himself from his previous commitment, that he'd love to meet up with her for supper.

But he didn't.

On the Monday morning, Bill paid another visit to the BWOC office. Determined to be organised about the after-dinner speaking possibilities Sal had mentioned, he decided he was going to build up a file of suitable 'by way of contrast' lines. The facility with which he'd remembered so many, in what he now recognised had been a chat-up routine with Maria, encouraged him. So did the reaction the lines had received at Sal's dinner party.

His spirits were high that morning. The varied responses to his encounter with Maria had settled down into a warm glow. Bill Stratton had been rehabilitated as a sexual player. The world was full of new possibilities. And old possibilities, he thought as he entered Carolyn's world of cigarette smoke, sweet tea and Radio 2.

The fullness of her body looked more attractive than ever. What Andrea had described as her 'obvious sexuality' was, that morning, very obvious. And yes, all right, her brassiness was obvious too. Bill knew he'd never be mad enough to come on to Carolyn, but he enjoyed his awareness of her sexuality.

She also seemed aware of the change of him. Was he being paranoid to detect a new knowingness in her blue eyes, as she said, 'You're looking very bright-eyed and bushy-tailed this morning'?

'You're looking good yourself.'

It was the first time in their relationship that he had complimented Carolyn on her appearance. Perhaps his new self was more relaxed about that kind of thing.

Not an easy woman to flatter, she snorted back, 'Yeah, but I don't look like you, not like I'm the cat that got the cream.'

The possibility that she did know about him and Maria could not be ruled out. Carolyn knew Sal. They hadn't met many times, but had talked a lot on the phone, coordinating the BWOC books and promotion. Had there already been a phone call between them that morning?

On balance, Bill thought it unlikely. He was just so conscious himself of what had happened that, in spite of four showers since the event, he still felt as though he reeked of sex. And he felt rather proud of the fact.

'I can look cheerful if I want to,' he riposted lightly. 'I just have a natural sense of well-being.'

'Oh yeah? With most men I've known, they only get that Cheshire Cat grin when they've had their oats.'

Surely she didn't know? Did she?

Deftly, Bill turned the conversation round. In the past he wouldn't have responded to Carolyn's frequent innuendoes. Now he felt empowered to do so. 'And would that explain why *you're* looking so bright this morning?'

But any thought that the enquiry might bring him information about Carolyn's sex life was doomed to disappointment. Expelling a derisive puff of air from her mouth, she said 'I've done with men, thank you very much', before continuing, 'Right, so presumably these BWOCs you want are going to be in different categories, according to the kind of audience you're speaking to . . . ?'

Chapter eight

. . . and, by way of contrast, in the recent Bristol West by-election, the candidate for the More Sex For All Party lost his deposit.

The after-dinner speaking bookings flooded in.

So did the dinner invitations.

And the number of Bill Stratton's sexual encounters increased too. He may have missed out on the sixties' Summer of Love, but he certainly enjoyed the Indian summer of his own sixties.

He thought of them as 'sexual encounters' rather than anything else. He certainly didn't think of them as 'conquests'. A 'conquest' suggests the subjugation of one participant by another, and all of Bill Stratton's sexual encounters were consensual. He couldn't see the attraction of any other kind of sex. He may have had a bit of the atavistic male rapist in him when younger, but now found sex no less satisfying, but less urgent. It was all a lot simpler at sixty.

Any seduction involved was verbal. He didn't make passes, he didn't put unsanctioned hands on thighs or breasts. When he met a woman he fancied and he seemed to be getting on with, he would gently ease the conversation towards talk of sex. If he got no response, he'd move back to less controversial topics.

But when the response came, he would tease the talk onwards, until some kind of agreement was reached. The negotiations, he knew, could always break down at the last minute, and sometimes they did. But at such moments his reaction, which in his youth would have been an agony of seething frustration, was now mild disappointment.

The sex itself sometimes worked, and sometimes didn't. But usually it was at least interesting. And Bill Stratton, having spent most of his adult life with one woman, came to realise how much he liked women as a gender, how much he enjoyed being in the company of women.

What he remembered about sex from his minimal premarital experience was the difficulty of finding opportunities to do it. He thought back to a time of constant frustration, when he didn't have a flat or even a car, when parents proved obstinately determined not to leave the house for any length of time, when bus shelters were too public and golf courses too wet.

But now, for a single adult, the opportunities were infinite. Most of the women he coupled with in London were single too, with homes of their own. When he was travelling round the country doing his after-dinner speaking, his contract always provided him with that philanderer's essential, a hotel room.

And of course, his own flat was permanently available. But he never took any of the women back there. He didn't want them to know about his domestic life. Despite being recognised as a minor celebrity, he wanted to preserve an element of anonymity.

The fact that his life had become a sequence of one-night stands caused him little guilt. The majority of the women with whom he shared his enthusiasm were equal players and wanted no more. Often divorcées, they were as wary of 'relationships' and 'commitment' as he was. Yes, there was the occasional tear or harsh word, but they were the exception.

And Bill Stratton deeply felt that he deserved a lot of sex. He remembered seeing a television interview with John Betjeman towards the end of his life, in which the old reprobate, asked if he had any regrets, stated the plaintive wish that he might have had more sex. Bill Stratton never wanted to find himself in that position. Only once he was out of his marriage to Andrea did he realise how much he had felt cheated of his part in the sixties sexual revolution. He had a right to as many lovers as possible before age finally took its toll, before the descent of that final shutter which would indicate the end of all sexual activity.

Bill was also surprised by how easy it was. After his 'Should we?' moment with Maria, he suffered no more such qualms. The shoulds and should-nots which once ruled his life had lost their potency. Finally, he felt grown-up.

He knew that not all his friends would agree with his definition of maturity. Though he felt confident it wasn't, his behaviour might be seen by some as predatory. Sal would psychoanalyse the hell out of him for seeking sex rather than 'relationships'. Carolyn would shake her head wearily at further confirmation that 'you men are all the same.' And Ginnie . . . he tried to shut his mind to conjectures about what Ginnie might think.

The way he avoided hearing such unsolicited opinions about his rediscovered sex life was by the simple expedient of telling nobody. And that went for male friends as well as female. He knew that some men liked nothing better than to share details of their conquests with others, but to Bill the idea of spilling the beans to someone like Trevor was anathema. He liked to think his reticence was a point of honour, an unwillingness to make public the names of ladies with whom he had shared an intimate moment. But really he knew that such self-justification was casuistry.

Remarkably, even in London, his policy of not going to bed with any woman more than once had not led to any embarrassing subsequent encounters. Dinner parties to which he was invited always tended to be in different circles of acquaintances. Being an unattached presentable straight male was valuable currency in London social life.

He was also fortunate that the women he chose — or who chose him — seemed to have the same desire for discretion. Which suited him fine.

He was sure this was partly because of their age. Though like all men, he could be turned on by the sight of a pretty young actress on television or in a movie, what appealed to Bill Stratton was his own generation of women. He fancied the women he should have been making love to in the late sixties, when he should have been sowing his wild oats. Meeting Andrea had consigned those wild oats to rot away in the large barn of marriage, but now he lusted after the women he had missed out on, the women he should have had, the women who were his by right.

So almost all of his bed-mates were around his age or older. Despite occasional wistfulness for the resilience of young flesh, he found mature women infinitely attractive. Maybe having lived with Andrea all that time, having watched her body imperceptibly change, made him more forgiving of the flaws of age. The glazed cotton of young skin might have turned to muslin, but it was still warm, the touch of flesh remained unique. Hands might be veined and freckled, but they could still hold and caress. For the first time he encountered stretch-marks, the silver flashes of unknowable experience. Like old houses, older women's bodies wore their quirky histories with a pride that he found more appealing than the slick convenient brand-newness of a starter home.

And then there were their eyes; infinitely various, infinitely wise. The eyes of young women had a bland, anonymous beauty; it was the surrounding wrinkles that created character.

There was also a basic fairness about Bill Stratton. How could he possibly blame women for the changes time had wrought on their bodies, when it had worked the same malign magic on his? Whitening hair, prominent veins and general sagging had caught up with him. What right had he to criticise their other victims?

One of the big advantages older women possessed was that they were knowledgeable about sex. Procreation or the prevention of procreation had long since ceased to be relevant; the only purpose of sex was to achieve pleasure. The potentially coy ones dropped out early in the course of mutual chat-up. Those who stayed the course revealed themselves to be at least as keen on a sexual encounter as Bill himself. They knew what they wanted, and they weren't afraid to instruct him on how to help them achieve it. As a result, Bill Stratton's sexual technique improved beyond recognition. He was a diligent and generous pupil, ready to pass on to his next partner the benefits of what he had learnt from the previous one.

And, though he wouldn't have been so crude as to subscribe to the line that 'it's better to make love to older women because they're so grateful', he was pleased that his efforts usually seemed to be appreciated.

He rather suspected his current life-style could not last for ever, but he felt no qualms about it. And had anyone asked him to explain his behaviour, he might well have used the justification of that great arbiter of contemporary morals, Bill Clinton . . . 'Because I could'.

'Could' in Bill Stratton's book, was a great improvement on 'should'.

Varied and wonderful were the sexual encounters of his period of freedom.

'Bill, that was stunning.'

'Thank you, Rachel. We aim to please.'

'Oh God!' Her hand leapt to her mouth. 'I haven't taken my pill!'

'But surely you're, er . . . well, not to put too fine a point on it . . . at your age . . .'

'Not that. Blood pressure.'

'Ah.'

'Cheryl, you're insatiable.'

'No, I'm not, Bill. I can be satisfied.'

'Oh?'

'By the right person.'

'Ah.'

'Sheila, was that from a car crash?'

'No. Hip replacement.'

'And, by way of contrast, let's try *this*.'
'Ooh . . . Celia!'

He never stayed the night. Some of the women claimed they wanted him to, but most made no demurral when he left. Partly, they had learnt by experience, and that was what they expected of men. And partly, they were realistic about the unforgiving focus daylight might bring to their charms. God is merciful, as we get older — he gives us failing eyesight, together with the instinct to take our glasses off in bed. But He still hasn't managed to fix the way we look in the cold light of day.

Bill knew, anyway, that his magnetism was finite. He didn't want to stay the night with any of the women. He didn't want to risk getting too close to what he thought of as his 'GCD.' In Bill's mind 'GCD' stood for Guaranteed Charisma Duration. It's the length of time for which a man can still stay attractive to a woman who doesn't know him that well. In other words, it's how long he can stay fiendishly witty/charming/caring/fantastic in bed. The length of time before he becomes tired/selfish/thoughtless/short-tempered/sexually-drained/himself. The length of time during which the magic of a relationship can be sustained . . . in other words, until he needs a shave, a fart or a crap, just like every other man she's met before.

Bill was punctilious, though, about his expressions of gratitude. Even when the sex hadn't been that good, a graceful message of thanks was always conveyed. And, having tried it out satisfactorily on Maria, he saw no reason to change the formula in which the message was expressed. His online Interflora account was kept busy. Nor did he bother to think up a new form of words to accompany the flowers. 'And, by way of contrast, thank you for an unforgettable experience.' It sounded all right, it was gracious, and it reminded the woman that she'd been made love to by a minor celebrity. So far as he was concerned, the flowers closed the transaction. The moment he'd given the woman thanks for an unforgettable experience, he was at liberty to forget her as soon as possible.

Bill was generally very impressed by the efficiency of the Interflora website, though from his point of view it did have one flaw. The service would remember a customer's credit card details, and an address list of the recipients of the customer's floral gifts, but it didn't have a memory for the messages sent with each bouquet. Bill Stratton would have found that a convenience. But it seemed to be a service for which there wasn't a demand. Most Interflora customers, Bill was forced to conclude, sent different messages to different people.

And, in his late-flowering promiscuity, did Bill Stratton himself change? Very little. Oh, he visited the gym more often. He had no illusions that he would ever recapture the physique of a young, muscle-bound Adonis (which he had never had), but since his body was going to be on display, he tried to ensure there was as little of it as possible. He wasn't obsessive about fitness, though. He didn't need to be. Nobody was going to see that much. Generally speaking, the women who shared his sexual encounters were even keener on muted lighting than he was.

The one big change he made was to his underwear. He found the small black briefs, variations of which he'd worn throughout his married life, were greeted too frequently in bedrooms with suppressed giggles. In boxer shorts he felt less tethered, but they did get fewer laughs . . . which was actually strange to Bill, because when he'd been growing up, the only times he'd seen boxer shorts were in American cartoons, on men who were meant to look funny in them.

And as for negative feelings — the suspicion that there might be something rather sad about a sixty-year-old man whose relationships were reduced to sexual scalp-counting — he managed to force such thoughts out of his mind. Bill Stratton had always been good at forcing unwelcome thoughts out of his mind.

Chapter nine

. . . and, by way of contrast, an eighteen-year old woman in Macedonia has been granted a divorce from her ninety-seven-year-old husband on the grounds of his unreasonable sexual demands.

Bill Stratton did not let his sex life impinge on his friendships. He still saw Carolyn at the BWOC office, had lunches and the occasional dinner party with Sal, and downed mournful pints in The Annexe with Trevor — but he never mentioned his sexual encounters. Carolyn probed with her customary innuendo. Sal — in her Miss Fixit role — tried to set up new trysts and get the low-down on old ones. But it seemed to Bill that he had no difficulty in deflecting their enquiries. And, of course, Trevor was no problem. Like most men, he was entirely uninterested in anyone's sex life but his own. Since that appeared to be moribund, he just maundered on about his past failures with women, which, transformed in the telling, increasingly took on the form of past glories.

And Ginnie . . . Bill didn't see much of Ginnie during that period. She had taken over the part of Mother Superior in a long-running television series about medieval nuns that was shooting in Croatia, where the cheapness of locations and labour made recreating the England of the Middle Ages much more attractive to television producers than it would have been in England. As a result, Bill and Ginnie had little contact other than snatched telephone conversations when she briefly touched base back in London. Bill was, in many ways, quite relieved about that. He had no problem in keeping his sex life secret from his other friends; he didn't know, though, whether he'd be able to withstand interrogation from the famous hazel eyes of Virginia Fairbrother.

There was no curiosity about his new lifestyle from his ex-wife. Andrea showed no interest in him at all. Occasional necessary phone-calls about final financial details were conducted quickly, without animosity, but neither of them volunteered information about themselves. Presumably, Andrea was enjoying Muswell Hill and domestic vegetarian bliss in the company of Dewi, which brought with it a licence for unbridled whingeing about the NHS. She had reached her nirvana.

Only once did Bill feel tempted to share some of the secrets of his new emancipation. And that was, surprisingly, with Trevor. They were sitting in the inevitable Annexe, and Trevor was working through his inevitable depression about how old he felt.

'. . . and you keep asking yourself, "What's the point?" Why should one go on when there's nothing left to look forward to? I mean, I see my body decaying by the minute. Every morning there are more dead, irreplaceable hairs on my pillow. My teeth feel more brittle every time I brush them. The veins on my legs look like the Piccadilly and Metropolitan Lines have taken over the entire tube map.' He took a long swig of beer, luxuriating in his misery. 'Even this is having less effect. It takes more booze to dull the pain, and the more booze you have, the more pain you feel when you wake up the next morning, which means you need even more booze to . . .' He sighed with satisfaction at the completeness of his despair. 'And there are so many things you just know you're never going to achieve . . . so many ambitions that will never be realised . . . I mean, I used to dream of being alone in a bedroom with a girl in her twenties . . .'

And as Trevor lifted his unfocused gaze towards his beer-tinted horizon, Bill Stratton felt really tempted to say, 'Actually, I've done that . . .'

But of course he didn't.

Not least because he did feel a degree of embarrassment about the whole episode.

The younger woman was encountered at a book launch. She worked, in some capacity Bill never quite established, for the company which had taken over his original publisher. (The enterprising young publisher who had seen the potential of the *By Way of Contrast* books had, in the way of enterprising young publishers, sold out to one of the big publishing conglomerates. He kept some minor advisory role in the business, but mainly he just enjoyed spending the huge amount of money he had made from the deal. And in the way of big publishing conglomerates, the big publishing conglomerate which had bought his company for its flexibility, low overheads and ability to react quickly to the market, proceeded to make their new purchase inflexible, to increase its overheads, and make it as slow to react to the market as all the other publishing houses under its umbrella.)

The girl's name was Kirstie, and her job

was something to do with 'rights'. Rights in what, or whose rights, or rights to do what, Bill never did find out. But she seemed happy to chat to him at the launch. She said she vaguely recognised him from the television, from when she used to 'watch with her parents'. Bill wasn't very good at judging the ages of people younger than himself, but he reckoned she couldn't yet have reached thirty.

The conversation followed a predictable format. He entertained her with some of his well-remembered 'by way of contrast' stories, in the constant expectation that she would shortly move away to join some of her contemporary colleagues. But she didn't. She seemed more than happy to stay listening to him, and they were still together when the trickle of departing guests became a gush. Asking her to join him for a bite to eat seemed an entirely logical next step.

They'd both had quite a lot to drink at the launch, and they continued to drink throughout their dinner at a convenient nearby Italian. Precisely the sequence of words that led to Kirstie suggesting that they should adjourn afterwards to her flat Bill could not remember. But again, logic seemed to be on their side. The idea made perfect sense to both of them.

As soon as the cab deposited them outside her block it was clear that Kirstie had a private income. Nothing anyone did with publishing rights would earn enough to pay for a flat in that neighbourhood of Fulham. Rich parents would be the probable explanation, but Bill didn't ask. He had no wish to hear that the girl's parents were younger than he was.

The interior of the flat confirmed the impression of wealth. So, now Bill came to think of it, did Kirstie's vowels. Their cut glass had been engraved to a very expensive standard by all the right schools.

She gestured him to a large white sofa while she disappeared into the kitchen to find yet more wine. Alone, Bill was able to take in his surroundings.

His first impression was that he was in a child's playroom. Carefully displayed on purpose-built shelves all around the walls were figurines of characters from Disney cartoons. He recognised the line-ups from *101 Dalmatians*, *Fantasia* and *Snow White*. All those bloody dwarves, of whom no one can ever remember more than six at any one time. Even with the seven little figurines in front of him, Bill couldn't get all the names right. He gazed around in bewilderment. Surely no one would actually *choose* to have this stuff on display?

'I see you're looking at my collection,' said Kirstie, returning with the wine.

'You collect these?'

'Well, don't say it like that. What did you think — that someone dumped them on me?'

That had been so close to what he'd been thinking that he didn't dare make any response. But Kirstie didn't need any; she was keen to talk about her hobby.

'My *101 Dalmatians* set is almost complete.'

'Ah, really?'

'Yes. That "Cruella in Bed" is terribly rare. It's one from the Walt Disney Classic Collection, obviously.'

'Obviously,' he echoed.

'And those "Puppies on Newspaper"?' Kirstie trilled. 'How sweet are they?'

Bill decided that this was a rhetorical question. He had been aware recently of a new syntactical interrogative creeping into the speech of younger people. Enquiries taking the form 'How good is that?' did not apparently expect answers. Bill didn't understand the grammatical construction, he was just aware of it. All he knew was that if he had used that kind of sloppy speech in his newsreading days, he would have got letters.

Still, Kirstie's collection did seem a viable topic for conversation. He couldn't spend the entire evening quoting 'by way of contrast' lines at her. And the brief forays they'd made over dinner into popular culture had not been encouraging. She knew the names of the Beatles and the Rolling Stones, but only as a shorthand for a state of embarrassing geriatricity. And her own musical favourites were equally unfamiliar to Bill. In fact, only the context made him realise that she actually had been talking about musicians. The names of the acts could otherwise have been mathematical formulae, firms of estate agents or skin infections.

And there had been an awful moment when he had managed to flood Kirstie's face with bewildered disbelief by asking her how often she went to discos. By the time he'd realised that the right word was 'club', he'd decided that music was probably a good subject to keep away from.

The cinema had proved over dinner to be an area of similar mutual incomprehension. Bill enjoyed films, but chose what he went to with care. He always based his decision on reviews by critics whom he respected. Whereas Kirstie appeared to be influenced only by a film's pre-release hype. As a result, her cinema diet consisted of worthless comedies with pretty boys in them, failed attempts to launch the Hollywood careers of American sitcom stars, mindless blockbusters full of special effects and — worst of all — inevitably inferior remakes of movies which had been perfect the first time round. Though he'd never seen any such films, Bill Stratton knew them all to be meretricious rubbish. He decided to keep off cinema as a subject for discussion.

So, though Kirstie's collection of china figurines may have been inspired by cartoon films, they still provided an innocuous topic. Chiefly because Bill had no opinion about them at all (except the vague conviction that they were rather hideous), and because Kirstie seemed prepared to go on about them at great length. Until that evening, he had not known that a world of collectibles existed, nor the passion and energy that a true *aficionada* could invest in trawling endless websites for the vital piece of china that would complete a set.

So he dozily sipped his wine, and issued the occasional sympathetic grunt when she explained the difficulties of tracking down *Beauty and the Beast* busts, the 'Limited Edition of Cinderella's Dress', or a 'Holiday Goofy with Cello Ornament'.

This conversation — or rather, mono-logue — only lasted the duration of one glass of wine, but it felt longer. Then, de-ciding that he'd misinterpreted Kirstie's in-tentions for the rest of the night, Bill took an elaborate look at his watch, yawned and said, 'Well, perhaps I'd better be off.'

But then she threw him totally by asking, in a slightly disappointed tone, 'Aren't we going to go to bed together?'

'Well, yes, all right.' As he said the words, Bill realised they could have sounded a little more gracious or enthusiastic. Nor did he feel the situation was entirely retrieved by his adding, 'If you like.'

Still, his clumsy response didn't appear to worry Kirstie. 'I'll get the wine bottle. You go through to the bedroom.'

She was a long time getting the wine bottle. Maybe she was also making some in-timate feminine preparations in one of the flat's bathrooms. Bill sat gingerly on the edge of the bed, wondering whether he was expected to start taking his clothes off. He decided against the idea, unwilling to expose his ageing body earlier than was strictly necessary. There were rather more lights on than he might have wished.

Feeling something of a prat, he just looked around the room, which was a shrine to *Bambi*, *Beauty and the Beast* and *Winnie the Pooh*. This last collection was displayed on a shelf above Kirstie's double bed. To Bill, who'd grown up with them, E.H. Shepherd's original illustrations were sacrosanct, and the crude Disney versions of the characters were as great an aesthetic affront as *The New English Bible* had been to *The Authorised Version*. But that was another opinion ideally not to be shared with Kirstie.

As he waited in this Temple of Disneyana, Bill didn't really feel lust. Just curiosity.

When Kirstie returned and kissed him gently on the lips, she smelt of fresh perfume and tasted of toothpaste, proving that she had indeed titivated herself up for him. He wondered with mild anxiety what, after the evening's drinking and the Italian food, his own breath smelt like.

Still, he couldn't bother about that. There was kissing to be done. And Kirstie did seem extremely keen on kissing. As their bodies stretched out together on the bed, lust returned, and a bit of fumbling with clothes began.

Kirstie drew apart from him. 'We'll be more comfortable in bed,' she announced practically. And then, thank the Lord, she switched off the overhead lights.

Bill stayed seated to remove his shoes and socks. He had reached the time of life when perfect balance could not always be guaranteed, particularly after an evening of wine. Already uncomfortably aware of his age, he didn't want to compound the stereotype by falling over.

Kirstie's clothes were off, and she was under the duvet, whither he crept, with some relief, to join her. For this encounter, he was really glad he had made the transition to boxer shorts.

He looked deeply into her eyes, then realised he still had his glasses on. Deciding clear vision must be sacrificed to avoid the laughable image of a bespectacled naked man, he took them off. He wished Kirstie too had glasses to take off, so that she'd only get a fuzzy outline of his ageing body.

'Have you got one with you?' she asked suddenly.

'Er, I'm sorry . . . what?' This confused him. Basic sex — the kind of sex they were about to indulge in — surely didn't need any props?

'A condom.'

'Ah.'

'Do you have one with you?'

'Erm . . . no, actually.'

When he considered the matter, it was remarkable that the question had not arisen before. There were enough earnest newspaper articles and television documentaries about safe sex. Primary school children seemed to be taught condom use before they were taught their alphabet. And all this earnest advice repetitiously pointed out the condoms were not just mandatory for their contraceptive properties, but also as a means of avoiding infection.

And yet not one of the women with whom Bill Stratton had made love during his post-Andrea flowering had mentioned the word condom. None of them had been at risk of pregnancy, but equally none of them knew his sexual history. The first post-AIDS panic seemed to have died down. The fierce questioning about previous partners which had happened then, when a potential lover virtually had to get planning permission for each sexual encounter, seemed to have become less urgent. Certainly none of the women with whom Bill had conjoined recently had mentioned the idea of his taking a medical before congress. Or of wearing a condom.

Probably a generational thing, he decided. For his contemporaries, condoms still had wartime connotations. They were 'Johnnies' or 'French letters', devices to protect our brave but randy boys from disease-ridden foreign whores. For the original post-pill generation, they were slightly distasteful. People whose first experiences had happened in the sixties didn't like the idea of having their sex shrink-wrapped.

The average heterosexual of his generation, Bill concluded, was extremely irresponsible about safe sex.

Kirstie's questioning did prompt another thought in him, though. She regarded him as a procreational threat. He couldn't remember when he'd last seen himself in that role. In the very early days of his marriage he'd entertained the possibility of Andrea becoming pregnant, but since then sex for Bill had been totally separate from the idea of reproduction.

Good heavens, he still had within him the capacity to become a father! He'd read somewhere that the sperm men produced declined in quality as they got older, but it still worked. Charlie Chaplin, Saul Bellow, Des O'Connor . . . there were a whole lot of men who had become fathers at very advanced ages. Hmm. When Bill reflected on those names, he decided it was not a club that he particularly wanted to join.

'It's all right,' said Kirstie resignedly. 'I've got some.'

The readiness with which she found the packet in her bedside drawer showed how well equipped she was for life as a single woman in the early part of the twenty-first century. Deftly, she popped a latex circle out of its foil and placed it on top of the unit. 'For when we need it,' she said, and leant forward to kiss him.

The kissing was again very pleasant and gentle. So was the caressing. With a slight feeling of guilt towards his other post-Andrea women, Bill couldn't be unaware of the superior skin quality he was now touching. He began to understand why so many men worshipped at the shrine of the younger woman.

During what he hoped would turn out to be foreplay, Bill couldn't prevent his eyes from wandering to the shelf above the bed. Eeyore looked down at him disapprovingly. He didn't let himself be put off by that. Eeyore disapproved of everything. In the Eeyore catalogue of unacceptable behaviour, making love to a girl less than half one's age was no more reprehensible than Kanga losing Roo, or Tigger bouncing. Bill still wished he was looking, though, at E.H. Shepherd's definitive images, rather than these winsome Disneyfied travesties.

The purposeful movement of Kirstie's

hands distracted him from nostalgia. 'I think maybe we need that protection now,' she said.

This was a new challenge. Though Bill Stratton was familiar with the concept, he had never actually put a condom on. And of course the important thing about putting a condom on is that there has to be something for it to be put on, and he found that, the nearer the point of putting it on came, the less there was to put it on.

Panic began to flicker in his brain. Remarkably, in his recent glut of sex, the one thing he hadn't encountered had been personal malfunction. Oh God, and it has to happen now, when I'm with a younger woman, a woman who spends her life surrounded by her contemporaries, men who go through life in a permanent state of semi-arousal. All the jokes he'd ever heard about old men not being able to get it up stampeded into his mind.

But Kirstie proved a surprisingly sympathetic and generous sex therapist. From what she said, this was by no means the first time she had encountered such a problem. As vigour returned to him, a marginal sense of superiority came with it. Maybe young men of Kirstie's age weren't such stallions, after all.

After the initial hiccup, everything proceeded smoothly. Bill Stratton's first sex with a condom definitely felt different, a bit remote even, but it was perfectly satisfactory. And Kirstie's responses seemed to suggest she got something out of the experience too.

After a mumbled 'Thank you', Bill lay in silence beside her, his mind full of the automatic masculine post-coital question. How soon can I leave? Books of etiquette are sadly inadequate in defining the recommended time-lapse between an act of intercourse and the first 'Oh, well, I'd better be on my way.'

But here too Kirstie surprised him. And anticipated him. With a brisk look at her watch and a 'Got to be at work in the morning', she made it quite clear that Bill's cue to get dressed had arrived.

There was no resentment or edge in her tone, just practicality. She put on a bathrobe and he quickly dressed. As he did so, he found his mind focusing on Kirstie's motivations. Was this how all of her sex life was conducted? Was it all quick pick-ups and goodbyes? Wham-bang-thank-you-sirs? And, most of all, why had she picked him? He'd been quite willing to go along with the scenario, but everything that had happened had been on her initiative.

Politely, she led him out through the sitting room.

'That was really nice,' he said. 'Thank you.'

His words sounded pretty flat, but they would be reinforced the next day by an Interflora bouquet with a note reading, '. . . and, by way of contrast, thank you for an unforgettable experience.'

'That's all right,' said Kirstie. 'I've never had an old man before.'

As he looked at the figurine-loaded shelves of her sitting room, Bill Stratton knew exactly where he fitted into the scheme of things.

And he decided that in future he'd stick to women nearer his own age.

Chapter ten

. . . and, by way of contrast, a recent survey in Canada has revealed that thirteen per cent of married couples had stopped having sex because they couldn't think of anyone else to think about while they were doing it.

Bill would have been lying if he said all the sex was good. But it was all sex. Sex that was his due. Sex that he should have had in his twenties, when he had instead been putting everything into a marriage which ultimately had turned out to be worthless. 'Saving it for marriage' had been his mother's strong recommendation, but she had failed to warn him that investments can go down as well as up.

Meeting so many women — albeit on a superficial level — prompted Bill to think a lot about gender differences. He kept coming back to the same question. How different are women? And he kept coming back to the same answer. Bloody different. Any man who aspires to spend time with them had better recognise that early on.

First, there were the simple biological differences. Particularly, that strange business of menstruation. Which, remarkably, women don't find that strange. They make much less of a fuss about menstruation than men do. Men continue to find it bizarre, imagining how they would feel if their bodies were invaded in that way on a monthly basis. Whereas women behave as if it were . . . well, natural. But, with the women who shared Bill Stratton's sexual encounters, that was no longer a problem. The menopause had sorted it all out, and Bill found that in many ways a relief. He had quite enough to think about without unpicking the chronology of menstrual cycles. He remembered back to the days of his marriage when an entire weekend's plans could be dashed on a Friday night by the rustle of a cardboard box heard from the lavatory.

Also, he felt the menopause put men and women back on an equal footing, like when they were children. Basically, men have never understood menstruation, and never will. They spend the major part of their lives when they're dealing with women, thinking, 'Oh, I shouldn't upset her. She has/has just had/might be about to have . . . her period.' And they feel guilty. At least, Bill reckoned, the menopause restores a vaguely level playing field.

Must be odd, though, having that happen to you. Though, in one sense, women are luckier than men. They have the menopause as a sort of early warning system. ('Hello, dear, just a reminder that you're well into the second half of your life.') Nothing like that for the chaps. For men death is a total surprise. No signposts in the masculine life between puberty and senility.

Oh dear, and there were so many gender issues Bill Stratton didn't reckon he'd ever get the hang of. For instance, the fact that the end of menstruation didn't spell the end of female difference. The divide between the way men and women thought seemed to increase with age rather than diminish. Women's priorities remained totally at odds with those of men. For instance, women seem able to summon up infinite interest in relationships *per se*. Anyone's relationship. Relationships in the abstract. Whereas the only relationships men are interested in are their own. If the world were peopled only by men, one thing that would vanish pretty quickly would be Romantic Fiction. For that to work, the reader has to give a toss who ends up with whom. And men just don't.

Men's and women's fantasies too follow totally divergent paths. The trouble with men's fantasies is they're all so unrealistic. Most of them involve playing for England in some sport for which you never had much aptitude, and for which you're now far too fat and beat-up to be a contender. Whereas women's fantasies . . . encompass the possible. The romantically possible. It is just possible that you'd go to Greece and meet some stud so naïf and pissed that he'd think you're attractive. It is just possible that, after a divorce, you might find your true self by pressing olives in Tuscany.

Unlikely, but still possible.

And that's before you even open the can of worms labelled 'Sexual Fantasies'.

What are women's sexual fantasies about? One thing's for sure, Bill Stratton concluded. I bet they involve a lot more talking than men's sexual fantasies do.

But women's fantasies are really no odder than the realities of their lives. Although in his sexual encounters he'd always tried to keep conversation on a light-hearted level, Bill had inevitably heard a lot about other people's relationships. Everyone has baggage. And everyone over sixty has so much baggage that if they had to pay the excess, it would bankrupt them.

Not having children of his own to bring to the conversation, Bill managed to avoid the bulk of his women's whingeing about their offspring, but there was no such easy escape from the whingeing about the men in their lives. His sexual partners, almost by definition, were not in warm and totally fulfilling relationships. Most were divorced or separated. And, though they all said they didn't want to talk about their past and previous partners, very few of them could carry that intention through.

So Bill did hear rather more than he might have wished about ex-husbands and lovers. Though none were accused of actual domestic violence, the men, it has to be said, didn't get a very good press.

After the first few diatribes, Bill could quickly have filled in the blanks himself. The men had all started off all right, but they had changed. In many cases it was marriage itself which had changed them. Before the wedding they had been generous, loving, caring, but the minute the rings were on their wives' fingers, they were transformed. The mild-mannered Dr Jekyll was gone for ever, and the domestic tyranny of Mr Hyde prevailed. (The fact that so many of the women seemed to have endured bad relationships for such a long time reminded Bill of what Andrea had said about their own marriage. But surely he'd never been as thoughtless as the husbands these women described? Had he?) The effect getting married had had on these former husbands had been devastating. They had instantly become jealous, possessive and controlling. They had become watchful of their wives' every activity, and deeply resentful of any attempts they made to set up social or commercial ventures that didn't involve their husbands. The men had become acutely critical of their wives' appearance and home-making skills. Their sole aim in life seemed to have become the total undermining of their wives' confidence.

Bill heard the litany so many times, and the details tallied so exactly in each case, that after a while an irresistible fantasy developed in his mind.

His sexual partners were not talking about different husbands. For each of them, it had been the same one. That was what must have happened — all divorced women had been married to the same man.

Whoever the man was, he certainly got around a bit.

Chapter eleven

. . . and, by way of contrast, a man in Powys who thought he had been conducting a secret affair for twelve years was disappointed to find out that his local nickname was 'Jones the Adulterer'.

'I'm still right. You're angry about what Andrea did to you. I've just read this book called *Revenge: Relationship as a Blunt Instrument*. It divides men up into categories. You're a classic "Rebound Wrecker".'

'Except, Sal, what am I wrecking?'

'The feelings of all these women you're bonking.'

'For heaven's sake. I'm not hurting them. I'm being very nice to them, and they like it. None of them is any keener to have a sustained relationship than I am.'

'No? I've just read this book called *Sex Objections: 101 Legitimate Reasons for Women to Refuse Sex —*'

'But they're *not* refusing sex — that's the whole point. Nothing happens that isn't consensual.'

'Bill, Bill . . .' said Sal patiently, 'will you

allow me to finish? I was about to say that in this book it says that the worst offence in relationships is to forget that the other person is a human being. Even in the current state of feminist thinking, there is nothing more demeaning for a woman than to be used as a sex object.'

'I do not use them as sex objects!'

That had come out rather louder than he intended, and turned a few heads in the Turkish restaurant. Fortunately, though, most of the lunchers there were Turkish (a tribute to the place's authenticity), and had no idea what he meant.

Bill was still in a state of shock at Sal's revelation that she knew about his recent phase of promiscuity. Obviously, she had known about Maria, who had, as it were, started his balls rolling, but Sal appeared to know there had been others too. How? Come to that, if she did know what he was up to, why hadn't she mentioned it before?

Still, the how-did-she-know question was more important. He'd tackled her directly about it the first time she described him as 'a naughty boy'.

'One hears things, Bill.'

'That's not very helpful.'

'Look, I'm your agent. I make it my business to know about what my clients get up to.'

'Like how?'

'Okay, after you've done a gig, the organisers sometimes ring up to say that it went well.'

'Oh.' He felt rather gratified.

'More often, though, they don't ring.'

'Ah.' He felt less gratified.

'So I give them a call, just to see that, like, there weren't any disasters.'

'And do they often report disasters?' he asked, alarmed.

'No, no, no. Most of the time they're very happy with you. The fact that they don't ring means nothing's gone wrong. God, if there had been a disaster, I'd hear soon enough.'

He was sidetracked by curiosity. 'What sort of disasters do occur?'

'Drink, usually. I have one or two clients who have a tendency to take the dinner part more seriously than the after-dinner speaking part.'

'Oh.'

'But they tend not to get booked again . . . and pretty soon I stop representing them. So don't get any ideas.'

'But I've never —'

'No, no, your behaviour has always been exemplary in that department. Everyone's very pleased with what you do.'

'Ah.' Gratification returned.

'Nothing a mildly pissed audience likes better than hearing all those hoary old "by way of contrast" lines again.'

'Oh.' The gratification was diluted. 'Well, at least they're all genuine.'

'Yes, yes, yes.' She'd heard all this before. 'Your journalistic integrity remains intact.'

'So there aren't any criticisms of what I do then?'

'No.'

'Then what's the problem?'

'No problem. As I say, there are never any criticisms, but there sometimes are . . . sniggers.'

'Sniggers? What kind of sniggers?'

'Sniggers of the kind that go . . . "Oh yes, I think Mr Stratton had a very good evening. He looked set to have a pretty good night too." '

'Ah.'

'You asked how I knew you'd been leading a life of wild promiscuity. Now you know.'

'Mmm.' He was thoughtful for a moment. 'But nobody's complained?'

'You'd know if the woman had complained.'

'I wasn't talking about the women. I was talking about the organisers. As you know full well.'

'No, none of the organisers have complained. As I say, they just snigger.'

'But how do they know?'

'It's not very difficult. What thoughts go through the average prurient masculine mind when they see a man and a woman leaving a hotel bar together?'

'Well, yes, I suppose so.'

'Also, in a lot of cases, they're not surprised by what's happened.'

'How can they not be surprised? They've never met me. They don't know that I might be on the lookout for . . . erm. . . .' He came back to '. . . for a sexual encounter.'

'No, Bill, they don't know you, but quite often they do know the woman.'

'Oh. I hadn't thought of that.'

'I mean, I'm sure you think it's all the work of your amazing animal magnetism, but it does, as they say, take two to tango. The kind of woman who's an easy pick-up for a one-night stand has quite frequently done that kind of thing before.'

'Right.' Bill wasn't enjoying this downgrading of his amorous adventures. It was as if he were becoming equated with the kind of man who drank too much — 'not so good after lunch, you know.' He asked the next question. 'You're not saying you reckon they must all be scrubbers?'

Sal's navy-blue eyes looked steadily into his. 'I didn't use the word.'

'Hmm.' He took a long swallow of the dusty red Yakut wine. Sal did the same. Then he re-engaged his eyes with hers. 'So, if my recent behaviour is, as it seems, common knowledge . . . what effect do you think it's had on my image?'

'That's hardly my problem, is it? The bookings are still coming in. Mind you, if being a randy old goat was a disqualification for celebrities doing PAs and after-dinner speaking . . . well, there'd be hardly anyone left on the circuit.'

'All right, put it another way . . . what effect does your new knowledge have on the way *you* think about me, Sal?'

He didn't know what response he'd been expecting. Certainly not the one he got — a shrug and, 'Well, let's say it doesn't raise you in my estimation.'

He couldn't deny feeling a bit shaken by what Sal had said. Particularly the bits about his using women as sex objects and going for easy lays (he closed his mind to the word 'scrubber'). His own vision of what had been going on was much more positive . . . romantic even. He saw himself as the rather dashing lover, bringing a little sunshine into the women's clouded lives. But he wondered, after what Sal had said, whether he'd ever be able completely to recapture that self-image.

Still, Sal was a woman. Women had never been great advocates of male promiscuity. She might even be a bit jealous. There was an undoubted attraction between them. And she'd probably just read some book called *You Got to Hide Your Love Away: Necessary Pretences in Interpersonal Relationships*.

Bill could do without a woman's sniping. What he needed was some mindless male solidarity. He rang Trevor and fixed to meet that evening in The Annexe.

'And you really have given up sex?'

'I told you, yes. Or rather sex has given up on me. The bloody thing doesn't work any more.'

'But, Trevor . . . maybe if you met the right woman . . .'

'I've spent my whole bloody life trying to meet the right woman, and it hasn't done me any good. If I couldn't find the right woman when I was firing on all cylinders — or at least on the one important cylinder — then I'm hardly likely to meet her now I haven't got anything in the way of cylinders to offer her.'

'No, I meant that maybe the right woman might be able to make you change your lifestyle. . . . You know, someone who really cared about you could nurse you back to a more cheerful outlook on things . . . get you off the booze . . .'

'Doesn't sound like the right woman to me.' Trevor put a full-stop to the line with a long swallow of beer.

'So you reckon sex really is over for you?'

'Yes! I've told you — why do you keep asking? My body has penetrated its last female body — and a good thing too! You've no idea how much clearer my brain is since I've stopped thinking about women all the time.'

'So if your brain's empty of thoughts of women, what's come in to fill the void?'

Trevor took another long pull from his pint glass. It seemed an adequate answer.

'Don't you think back nostalgically to the women you did make love to?'

He shook his head. 'Never. Forgotten all of them.'

'You can't even remember how many women you have gone to bed with in your life?'

'No.' There was a long silence before Trevor said, 'Seventeen.'

'Ah.' Bill resorted to his pint.

'How about you?'

'Sorry?'

'How many women have you gone to bed with?'

Bill had a moment of fear. Did Trevor's question imply that he too knew about his friend's recent behaviour? After the bombshell from Sal, he was beginning to wonder whether details of his sexual encounters had been posted on some international website, so that there wasn't a person in the world unaware of them.

Cautiously he replied, 'Well, I spent nearly forty years only going to bed with Andrea.'

'That wasn't the question I asked. How many women have you gone to bed with?'

Bill was tempted. After a slow start, his total was now getting quite impressive. Certainly exceeding Trevor's. There was an atavistic masculine attraction in the idea of crowing over his friend. But then again, if Trevor didn't know about Bill's recent liaisons, maybe it'd be better for him to remain in ignorance.

'Oh . . .' Bill lied. 'I don't know.'

He had a brief moment of anxiety with Carolyn too. Something she said made him wonder about the confidentiality of his private life.

He had dropped into the BWOC office to pick up the latest haul of 'by way of contrast' lines. There was no necessity for him to do that; they could easily have been sent by email. But his visits were a regular part of his routine — one of the few elements of routine his life offered, apart from the round of PAs and after-dinner speeches. And being in the office as BWOC's director gave him the illusion of being part of a busy business life.

Also, he couldn't deny that he enjoyed being in the same room as Carolyn. Andrea, he was sure, had been right about her, but a little bit of 'obvious sexuality' never did anyone any harm. Being with Carolyn made Bill think of being in a bakery . . . and of other warm, rounded, fresh things. Of course he was never going to come on to her — he'd heard far too much of her cynicism about men to risk that kind of tongue-lashing — but he did find her presence comforting. As he found the whiff of tobacco and the warm sweet tea and the schmaltz of Radio 2 comforting.

She was talking about her son Jason, guru of the computer, creator and maintainer of the website which allowed BWOC to run with such painless efficiency. 'He could be making millions,' she was complaining, 'but what's he done? Only cut back on his IT work to concentrate on trying to become a stand-up comic.'

'But is he funny? He's always seemed rather serious when I've met him.'

'God knows whether he's funny or not,' she drawled throatily. 'He was funny when he was about three years old, but that's not the point. I made a lot of sacrifices to get him properly educated, and now he's turning down the chance to really clean up financially.'

'Still, if it's what he wants to do . . . surely, as his mother, you'd support any-thing he —'

'Sod that.'

'Ah. How is he otherwise?'

'Otherwise he's behaving like anyone else who had the good fortune to be born with a tassel. Like he owns the whole bloody world, at least as far as women are con-cerned.'

'No regular girlfriends then?'

'No, and far too many irregular ones. Jason doesn't go for quality, he goes for quantity. He's not going to commit himself to being responsible for a woman. He's a real "notches on the bedpost" man.' And then she said the words that gave Bill a little trickle of anxiety. 'Just like you.'

'Just like me?' How could she know? How could she possibly know? Maybe there actually was a website called 'billstrattonssexualencounters.com'?

But no, it must be through Sal. Carolyn and Sal had to talk from time to time about the *By Way of Contrast* books. That must be the source of Carolyn's knowledge. Oh God, the whole bloody world knew. Probably even Andrea and bloody Dewi knew, and spent evenings over tofu bakes with their NHS harpies castigating his moral character.

'Er . . . why do you say "just like me"?' Bill asked cautiously.

Her blue eyes x-rayed him. 'Because you're a man.'

Phew . . . nothing personal, just one of Carolyn's regular diatribes against his gender. He couldn't believe — and was rather surprised by — the level of relief that he felt.

Chapter twelve

. . . and, by way of contrast, a Salt Lake City Mormon with nine wives married one more so that he could get a discount on air travel.

The restaurant style this time was Moroccan *riad*. Tables on the ground floor, matched by those on the two galleries above, were set against the walls around a central fountain. A glass covering at the top of the space gave an illusion of openness to the sky. Multitudes of candles in spiky metal holders twinkled against engraved cedar doors and *zellij* tiles of deep blues and greens. Their light flickered over carved stucco, up tall pillars to ornately geometric friezes. Beautiful white-clad waiters flitted through the shadows. Rose petals were scattered over every surface.

'Bit over the top.' Virginia Fairbrother grimaced wryly. 'Ever since Marrakech was rediscovered by the B-list, this has been inevitable.'

'Have you been there?'

'Oh yes, Bill. Of course.' She looked around disparagingly. 'Don't know how

165

long this one'll last.'

'Is the food just straight Moroccan?'

'No, they couldn't charge these prices if it was. But the chef's wife's Japanese, so they reckon that adds some kind of fusion element to the cuisine. You can always charge more for fusion.'

'It was well written up in one of the Sunday papers.'

'Yes, but that's easily arranged. Invite the right people to the launch, you'll get the coverage. The difficult thing is to keep the right people coming when you're up and running.' She looked around at the other diners. Her expression indicated that the new restaurateurs had failed in their mission.

It had been a last minute arrangement. An unexpected break in the Croatian filming schedule, Ginnie had managed to wangle a flight, and she'd called Bill as soon as she got back to London. He'd very much wanted to see her, but wished it hadn't been the weekend when he was still feeling raw after Sal's revelations.

Still, Ginnie was looking stunning. Her hair was short, in deference to her role as a nun in the television series, but it was cut with consummate skill. The Croatian sun had topped up and burnished her tan to a new glowing splendour, perfectly set off by the white linen trousers and minimal pink silk top she was wearing.

'I never quite understand,' said Bill, 'why your hair has to be short if it's covered all the time.'

'Then you've clearly never seen the series,' purred Ginnie. 'Mine is very definitely a "wimple-off" role. The whole show is *Sound of Music* meets *Prisoner Cell Block H*.'

'I'm sorry. I should have seen it.'

'Quite honestly, darling, I'd rather you didn't. Rather a dilemma for me, actually. For the show to succeed, it needs millions of viewers. All I hope is that none of them are people I know. It's on ITV, though, so I'm in with a chance.' She shuddered. 'There is such a thing as actors paying their mortgages too publicly, and I'm afraid that's the situation I'm in. Still, nobody's doing anything mildly intelligent on television these days, and since the theatre work's virtually dried up . . .' she shrugged her magnificently slim shoulders '. . . beggars can't be choosers.'

She flashed him a sudden grin. 'Enough of my problems. Is your new career on the after-dinner circuit burgeoning?'

'Seems to be going all right. Don't know

why really. I mean, I say exactly the same things every time.'

'So? Bill darling, if you were an actor, no one would complain about that. When I gave my Lady Macbeth, I said exactly the same things every time. If I hadn't, the audiences would have asked for their money back.'

'Yes, but what I trot out is far from Shakespeare. I mean, they're genuine, but they're basically just tired old snippets of yesterday's news.'

'That's how they may appear to you, but what you have to remember is that that's not how the audience sees it. They're hearing it for the first time.'

'Suppose you're right.'

'Of course I'm right, Bill. Come on, this is not your usual perky self. Why're you down?'

'Erm . . .' He couldn't give the real answer. That being with her, realising how much he liked her, relaxing in the company of a real woman whom he knew well, made his sexual encounters of the last months seem a bit . . . well, tawdry. The lunch with Sal had planted the seed of self-disgust within him; being with Ginnie made it grow. 'I don't know,' he concluded unsatisfactorily.

'Something going wrong with your love life?'

'Good heavens, no,' he said, with too much vehemence.

'I hope you do have a love life . . .'

'Well . . .'

'When we last had dinner, you said you were still technically faithful to Andrea.'

'I didn't exactly say —'

'I do hope that's no longer true . . . for your sake. Remember all that ground you've got to make up.'

'Well . . .'

'Go on, Bill.' She leant forward, teasing, provocative. 'Tell me the truth. You've been picking up women and shagging them at every one of your after-dinner speaking gigs, haven't you?'

It was hopeless. They all knew. There probably was a 'billstrattonssexualencounters. com' website. Nothing for it. He'd have to bite the bullet.

'Yes,' he admitted sheepishly. 'Well, not at every one, but . . .'

Ginnie's indrawn breath and the change in her expression told him, too late, that he'd made a big mistake. She'd just been teasing him. She hadn't really thought he'd been picking up women and shagging them at every one of his after-dinner speaking gigs. Oh God, talk about having blown it.

'Joking,' he said hopefully. 'Just joking.'

But he could see she didn't believe him.

Mercifully the waiter arrived to take their orders. Ginnie went for a Berber Sushi Salad starter, followed by the inevitable Lamb Teriyaki with Apricots Tagine. Bill, at a loss to think about anything other than the gaffe he'd just made, asked for the same.

Any hopes he might have had of the waiter's interruption shifting the topic of conversation were dashed, as Ginnie went on, 'So . . . how many has it been?'

'How many?' he echoed feebly. 'How many what?'

'How many women have you shagged since your divorce from Andrea?'

'I don't know . . .'

'You mean you don't know because there've been so many you've lost count?'

'No. I don't know . . . because . . . well, it's not the kind of thing that one does count.'

'Nonsense. Men always count.'

The hazel eyes bored into him, but he wasn't going to tell her.

'So, Bill, you've suddenly become The Oldest Swinger in Town, have you? Joining the Rod Stewart and Peter Stringfellow Brigade?'

He was repelled by the image. 'No. Nothing like that. Anyway,' he said defensively, 'last time we had dinner together, you were encouraging me to get my sex life up and running again.'

'Yes, but I wasn't encouraging you to shag *everyone*.'

'I haven't shagged everyone.'

'Oh, goodness. You mean here and there a woman exists who has yet to receive the infinite blessing of your body?'

'Ginnie, I don't know why you're going on about it. Can't we talk about something else?'

'Possibly. In a minute. But not before I've got a little more detail about what you've been up to for the last few months.'

'Oh.' He looked glumly down at his right thumb and forefinger, which had been unconsciously rolling together rose petals. The debris of tiny broken red pellets lay on the tablecloth.

'Do I take it these were all one-night stands?'

A lugubrious nod.

'Nothing that you would term a relationship?'

Another.

'And don't you think that's rather irresponsible behaviour?'

That did surprise him. 'No. None of them were of an age when they were likely to get pregnant.'

'That's not the only kind of sexual irresponsibility, Bill. Don't you think there might have been an element of disloyalty in what you've been doing?'

'No. For heaven's sake, I haven't got anyone to be disloyal *to*. You seem to be forgetting that Andrea and I got divorced. While I was married to her, I was completely faithful. Now the marriage is over, I can do what I like. I don't have any responsibility to anyone.'

'Not even to the women you've had all these one-night stands with?'

'No.' He'd never really thought of that possibility. 'No. They weren't under any illusions. They were just like me, only in it for a quick sexual encounter.'

'God, Bill, you talk like an adolescent who's just discovered sex.'

'Well, maybe that's what I am.' He grinned, trying to get their conversation back on to its usual level of banter. 'As one keeps reading in the Sunday papers, "sixty is the new thirty".'

'In your case, sixty's more like the new sixteen. Come on, tell me . . .' The hazel eyes once again impaled him like a butterfly on a pin. 'Have you really enjoyed having this random sequence of quick screws?'

He certainly wasn't going to deny it. 'Well, yes, I have. Most of them. Anyway, I was due a few. You told me so when we last met.'

'Did I?'

'Yes. Your exact words, if I recall them correctly, were, "You don't have to marry every woman you have a relationship with." '

'But apparently you aren't having relationships with these women. You're just having sex with them.'

'It comes to the same thing.'

Ginnie looked at him, appalled, and slowly shook her head. 'Surely you don't believe that? Sex must mean something. Not just passionless promiscuity.'

'What's wrong with promiscuity?'

'It's not funny and it's not clever.'

'No, but it's FUN.'

Ginnie shook her head in disbelief. 'You just don't get it, do you, Bill?'

'Don't get what?'

'You must be so full of anger against women.'

'I'm not full of anger. I'm very nice to them. I give them a good time.'

She didn't seem even to hear that. 'I suppose it's your revenge for what Andrea did to you.'

'Oh, don't you start. Sal keeps saying that.'

'Sal your agent?'

'Yes.'

'Oh.' A new thought came to Ginnie. 'She isn't one of your conquests, is she?'

'Good heavens, no. I don't do it with women I *know.*'

Her expression made him wish that those words too had been left unsaid.

'What I mean is —'

'I know exactly what you mean, Bill, and I can't deny that I'm disappointed in you.'

'Oh, for heaven's sake, Ginnie, you're the last person I would have expected to go all moralistic on me. And I have to say there is an element of pot and kettle here. Your emotional history has been an unblemished record of fidelity, has it? You've had lots of lovers.'

'Yes, but they were *lovers.* There was *love* involved. I went into each relationship thinking it was going to work out. None of them were just anonymous carnal transactions.'

'You don't know that's what mine were.'

'If you only see any of the women once, that's very much what they sound like. One step up from using prostitutes, and with the big advantage that you don't have to pay.'

That stung him. Petulantly, he said, 'Look, I'm still recovering from my divorce. I'm not ready for a long-term relationship.'

'Oh, don't come that one with me, Bill.

174

God, you really are having a second adolescence. Most boys realise by their twenties how meaningless sex is without emotion. Most grow out of the "notches-on-the-bedpost" mentality.'

'For nearly forty years of marriage I didn't have a "notches-on-the-bedpost" mentality.'

'So that justifies your having one now, does it?'

Yes, it does. The response was instinctive, but he didn't vocalise the words. Ginnie had hit the nail on the head with uncomfortable accuracy. She had spelled out exactly what he thought.

Their Berber Sushi Salads arrived, but again the break didn't deflect the implacable Ginnie. 'I feel really sorry for you, Bill.'

'Well, that's very sweet of you, but you don't need to. I'm perfectly happy.'

'Are you, though? Listen, you're a nice guy —'

'Not from what you've been saying.'

'Yes, you are. And you've got a lot to give emotionally . . . which is why I'm so pissed off to hear that you're just playing a numbers game, ticking off the lists of your conquests —'

'They're not conquests. It's all consensual.'

'Huh. They must all be the same kind of women.'

'Maybe they are.'

'Well, thank God I'm not that kind of woman. I can't imagine anything more demeaning than being just another name in a man's point-scoring roll-call of lovers.'

That silenced him. Not because of the criticism, but because of the implication — however ambivalent and veiled — that there might be circumstances under which she would have contemplated being his lover. The idea was so potent it took his breath away. He wished even more forcibly that their recent conversation had never started.

Compassion had replaced anger in her voice, as Ginnie said, 'I just feel sorry that there's no love in your life, Bill. Perhaps no love in you.'

'That's hardly my fault,' he responded instinctively. 'I tried nearly forty years of love, and then discovered that it wasn't reciprocated.'

The hazel eyes looked pityingly at him. 'God, you're so angry.'

'Well, all right, maybe I am,' he conceded.

She shrugged. 'Oh, it's your life and . . . sorry, I shouldn't have come the heavy moralist with you. It's just . . . you're someone I care about, and so I want you to be happy.'

He didn't bother insisting again that he *was* happy. Ginnie had managed to devalue his idea of happiness. Instead, rather grumpily, he repeated, 'I'm just not yet ready for another relationship.'

'No, but you can still have some love in your life. It doesn't need to be exclusive love, like you had for Andrea. You can have love for friends, for people you meet. You should let yourself be open to love.'

'How do you know I'm not?' he asked truculently.

'I know. Serial philanderers shut off the possibility of love. Shagging lots of women is their way of immunising themselves against it.'

'Hmm. Maybe.'

'Come on, think. Isn't there anyone in your life for whom you feel a bit of love?'

There were people, but he didn't think it tactful to mention either Sal or Carolyn to Ginnie. Instead, boldly he said, 'I feel a bit of love for you.'

She grinned, reached across the table and put her hand on his. 'And I feel a bit of love for you. A bit.' She removed her hand. 'But rather less than I did at the beginning of the evening.'

Chapter thirteen

*. . . and, by way of contrast, a Bengali
woman accused of marketing a fraudu-
lent love potion was acquitted by a
judge, who subsequently married her.*

Bill Stratton could not deny that he was
shaken by what Ginnie Fairbrother had
said. Her perspective on his recent life did
make it appear slightly shabby. That, coupled with Sal's words about people 'sniggering', diminished his self-image as a
magnificent love-god. He was just another
more-than-middle-aged man, trying to
cram in as much action as possible before
the final shutter fell.

He was also intrigued as to why Ginnie
had taken him to task with such vigour. Fair
enough that she should disapprove of his
late-flowering promiscuity, but she seemed
to be taking it personally, as if it was her
he'd let down, rather than her entire gender.
Bill didn't allow himself to think why she
should have behaved like that. He just
wanted to see her again as soon as possible,
and find a way to reinstate himself in her
good books. But that was not going to be

easily achieved. The morning after their dinner she had flown back to Croatia, where she was scheduled for many more months of convent capers. Bill's bridge-building with Ginnie would have to wait. But he did think a lot about what she said. Particularly about the lack of love in his life. While he had been with Andrea — even though she subsequently denied its presence — he at least had had the illusion of love surrounding him. And it was true that love had not been a component in any of his sexual encounters since the divorce.

Men were, of course, proverbially bad at using the 'L' word. The commitment implied in it was so total. Telling a woman that you loved her was tantamount to signing a binding contract never to stop loving her, undertaking to protect and look after her for as long as you both shall live. Or at least that was the way Bill had always seen the situation. And he reckoned that was the reason why most men avoided all mention of love in their dealings with women. It was safer that way. But what Ginnie had said made him wonder whether his definition of love was perhaps too narrow. Ideal married love to one person was a nice idea, but how many people achieve that? Bill Stratton thought he had, but he'd been wrong.

Ginnie had hurt him when she said there was no love in his life. Maybe there wasn't that one exclusive love, but perhaps by a more relaxed definition . . . ? Well, he certainly felt something for Ginnie. That was a kind of love — he'd told her so. Perhaps he felt something similar for Sal, come to that. Even Carolyn.

Maybe he should tell them that he loved them? Mind you, he wasn't quite sure what response he would get. Baffled incomprehension, most likely.

Interesting idea, though. It might, he thought, be quite easy to say 'I love you', once he got used to the idea. Once he'd managed to break the habit of thinking in terms of exclusive love, just for one person. But when he'd done that, and when he'd actually said it to more than one person, well, maybe it'd be open season on 'I love you.' He could say it to anyone. The important thing, though, Bill told himself, mindful of Ginnie's criticisms, is that it's true. You only say it to people you love. But the number of those — and the different ways in which you love them — well, the older you get, the bigger that number might become.

He wished he'd been more forceful when he'd told Ginnie that he loved her. But he'd been on the back foot all that evening; not really a time for being forceful.

He supposed he could write to her or phone her. She'd made a point of telling him how well her mobile worked in Croatia. But he didn't want to put the delicate balance of their relationship at risk. Even when she gave him an ear-bashing, being with Ginnie meant a lot to him. Saying the wrong thing or making a wrong assumption about her interest in him could spoil everything. Virginia Fairbrother was a wonderful and attractive woman, but she was way out of his league.

A couple of days after their Moroccan/Japanese fusion experience, Bill Stratton had an after-dinner speaking engagement in a hotel in Nottingham. There was an unattached woman there who was giving all the signals of availability. They chatted in the bar afterwards. She laughed at his 'by way of contrast' lines and seemed in no urgency to leave. At about midnight Bill looked at his watch and said it had been a pleasure to meet her, but he must be off to bed.

Where he went. Alone. Feeling incredibly virtuous.

He found over the next few weeks that his mind kept coming back to things Ginnie had said to him. He wondered about the anger. Had he really been using promiscuity as a way of getting back at Andrea? Not directly, of course, because she knew nothing about what he'd been doing, but maybe there was something in the theory. Sal, after all, had said exactly the same thing. Bill also thought about Ginnie's description of him treating sixty as the new sixteen. He did feel as if he was going through a change in his life. Maybe, he wondered, second adolescence is a necessary stage before second childishness. And mere oblivion. His behaviour certainly couldn't be covered by the catch-all title of 'a mid-life crisis'. If this was his *mid*-life, then by the time he died he was going to have an entry in the Guinness Book of Records. But he did need a little time to reassess his situation. He was glad he'd done his stint as a serial philanderer, but that wasn't how he wanted to spend the rest of his life. As an old goat, being sniggered at by event organisers.

Maybe in future he should be on the lookout for more than sex. Possibly even for love.

When he next had lunch with Sal, he told her that he loved her. Their meeting had started rather oddly, because Bill knew there was something different about his agent, but he couldn't quite identify what it was. A disproportionately long time elapsed before he realised it was her smile. Ever since he'd known her, she'd had the yellowed teeth of a continually re-offending smoker; now suddenly he was faced with two rows of gleaming whiteness.

He didn't quite know what to say. It was a bit like seeing a bald man the first day he wears his toupee. Presumably he knows that he had no hair the previous day, and he knows that his colleagues know. New acquaintances might possibly be impressed and fail to notice that nothing on his head moves, but what is the recommended behaviour for old friends? Is the correct form to say nothing and pretend you haven't noticed? Or is it more polite to extend your hearty congratulations to him on the fact that he has suddenly got a large Shredded Wheat on his head? Sal's sudden orthodontic makeover presented Bill with a similar social dilemma.

But he needn't have worried. She *wanted* to talk about her new teeth. In fact, there was no way she was going to be stopped from talking about them.

'Porcelain veneers,' she said. 'Aren't they wonderful?'

'Yes. You look splendid.'

'Cost an absolute fortune.'

'I bet. All those fifteen per cents of my earnings.'

'Don't you believe it. Thank God I've got other clients. *You* only paid for that tiny little one at the back. Anyway, it's part of the new me.'

'Another "new me"? You're some kind of new you every time I see you.'

'Oh yes, in the past,' she conceded, 'I have gone for all kinds of self-help books, you know, trying to change my personality. But I've given up on that. Now I'm going to change the shell, and let the personality develop inside it.'

'By "the shell", you mean your exterior appearance?'

'Yes.'

'What, so you're going to wear more make-up?'

'I don't think that'd be possible.'

'Ah.' Light dawned. 'You mean you're going to change your body?'

'Exactly. The teeth are only the start. I'm having a consultation with a cosmetic surgeon tomorrow. Soon you won't recognise the new me.'

'Don't make too many changes,' he said. 'I really like the old you.'

'Yes, but that's what's wrong with it. It's old. Soon I'll be totally transformed.'

'Well, do be careful.' Then he added, boldly, 'I love the old you.'

She didn't seem to notice this avowal. If that's what it was. Certainly Bill had never used the word 'love' to Sal before. Without even registering the novelty, she started on at him about how he ought to get his teeth fixed too.

'You are in the public eye, you know. You've always got to look your best. It's a cut-throat business you're in. A lot of younger, better-maintained men out there, snapping at your heels.'

'Maybe, but I don't need cosmetic dentistry. My teeth are part of me. They've got a lot of character.'

'You could say the same of Stonehenge.' She looked disparagingly across at his uneven bite. 'And, actually, the similarities don't stop there.'

Bill didn't really like this talk about his teeth. They had always been sensitive, and he had always been sensitive about them. He had had a lot of trouble with them over the years, though now they were so full of fillings there wasn't much left that could go wrong with them. They probably could do with porcelain veneers, but he reckoned, having got this far into his life without them, the unadorned original teeth would probably see him out. And when he had been regularly reading the news, his 'crooked smile' had been referred to frequently. He'd even once had the accolade of his facial expression being mimicked by an impressionist in a television sketch show. Still, thinking about his teeth always upset him. Maybe because of their similarity to tiny tombstones, they made him aware of his own mortality.

Fortunately the conversation did at last move away from matters orthodontic. Sal was in very good form, seemingly liberated by the decision to lay off her mind and concentrate on improving her body. She was funny and relaxed, and they went for a second bottle of the dusty red Yakut. As they parted outside the Turkish restaurant, they went into a more effusive clinch than usual. Bill could feel the outline of her body against his. Clumsily kissing her hair, he mumbled, 'I do love you, you know.'

'I love you too,' she murmured.

Then, with a tipsy giggle, she tottered off on unfeasibly high heels back towards her office.

Sitting on the tube back to Pimlico, Bill Stratton glowed. Maybe there was love in his life, after all. He'd never really thought about fancying Sal, until that moment when she pressed her body against his.

So there was something between him and Sal . . . and definitely something between him and Ginnie. It was rather nice, the idea of being a little in love with more than one person. Suddenly he felt a huge surge of well-being, possibly buoyed up by having sunk a whole bottle of the Yakut. He felt the capacity to love every woman in the world. They were so gorgeous. The curves of their breasts and legs, the infinite variety of their skin tones, the way their hair sprang and curled and shimmered from their heads. At Green Park a woman of incredible beauty boarded the tube and stood opposite him. Probably under thirty, she had short blonde hair and honey-dappled skin. A short skirt and sleeveless top showed her perfect contours. Long, long legs, slender muscular arms, an immaculate cleavage.

The well-being within Bill Stratton surged again. She was so beautiful. He was instantly in love with her. And he wanted to tell her so, to let her know how much she was appreciated. Surely any woman would want to know that a man found her beautiful? Since they spend so much time and artifice trying to achieve that effect, they must want to be informed when they have succeeded. Bill decided he would tell the woman she was beautiful. He might even say that he loved her. The unsolicited opinion of a man of taste — that'd really give a lift to her day.

The tube was slowing down for Victoria and she started moving towards the door. That was why she hadn't bothered to sit down, she was only travelling the one stop. She was going to walk right past Bill, and when she did, he would stand up and tell her she was beautiful. And possibly that he loved her.

He timed it beautifully. He stood up when she was directly in front of him, and he opened his mouth to speak. But then he saw the expression which had taken over her beautiful face. The expression which only he could have inspired. Contempt and distaste, with an undercurrent of fear. Someone so beautiful got men coming on to her all the time. She loathed it.

Bill wanted to explain. That he wasn't a threat to her, he just appreciated her aesthetically. That he really wasn't coming on to her. That. . . .

It was over in a matter of seconds. No one else in the carriage saw the look of loathing that had passed from her to him. She was gone, the doors closed and the tube sighed on towards Pimlico. Bill Stratton slumped back in his seat and saw in the window opposite, in ghostly reflection — rather like an X-ray image — exactly what the young blonde woman had seen. A white-haired, wrinkled figure with irregular teeth. An old goat. A dirty old man.

Chapter fourteen

. . . and, by way of contrast, a new Christian society for teenagers has been founded in Ohio. It is called the Affirmative Response Group, and its slogan is 'Say No to Everything'.

Leigh was different from the other women, though the circumstances in which Bill met her were pretty similar. An after-dinner gig in London for some charity. Not that his own involvement was in any way charitable. Sal had sorted out a contract for his usual fee and his usual hotel room. So far as she was concerned — and so far, after brief initial qualms, as Bill was concerned — a booking was a booking. A charity could always try approaching a speaker direct and ask if he'd give his services for nothing. But if they went through Sal Juster Associates, they were by definition entering into a commercial transaction. (Many charity events — and particularly Charity Balls — actually lose money, because the initial outlay has been so huge that no amount of ticket sales or donations on the night are going to cover it. Enthusiastic people on charity committees rarely have much understanding of event finances. Still, that wasn't Bill Stratton's problem.)

He couldn't remember what that night's particular charity was; something to do with a heart scanner or a new hospital wing for sick babies. He took a perverse pleasure in not knowing the details. Being of a medical nature, it was one of the few such events at which Andrea might have joined him . . . had they, of course, still been married. Except, of course, had they still been married, he wouldn't have embarked on his career in after-dinner speaking, so he wouldn't actually have been invited to. . . . Such speculation was pointless.

Anyway, rather than Andrea, he met Leigh. She was tiny and vivacious, with that combination of very black hair, lightly freckled skin and pale blue eyes that ought to be Irish, though in her case apparently wasn't. She wore a trouser suit that looked black until the light caught it and made it shimmer with dark green.

The first thing that distinguished her from his other women was that she had not come to the function alone. Seated next to Bill on the top table at the dinner, she introduced him to a broad bald man with glasses on her right, who seemed to have been melted down and poured into a rigid dinner suit. Bill couldn't remember the man's exact name, but it was in the Keith/Derek/Alan range. Anyway, throughout the dinner, Keith/Derek/Alan seemed surplus to Leigh's requirements. She spent the whole meal listening to Bill, laughing appropriately at his well-remembered 'by way of contrast' lines. She laughed too as the BWOC routine was wheeled out during the actual speech, but when he sat down to his customary flurry of applause, she said, 'You don't give much of yourself away, do you?'

'What do you mean?'

'Lots of second-hand funny lines, nothing about the real Bill Stratton.'

'All the punters want is a laugh. They haven't come here to hear about the real Bill Stratton. Which is just as well, because the real Bill Stratton is not particularly interesting.'

'Difficult to know, since you won't reveal anything about him. I would have thought . . .'

Her words trickled away at an admonitory look from the event's chairman, who was about to start the evening's Auction of Promises.

In a much lower voice, she murmured, 'Let's go and have a drink at the bar.'

'Well . . .' Although he didn't have any role that evening as auctioneer, award-presenter or raffle-ticket-picker, slipping away straight after his speech was on the margins of bad form. And slipping away with a woman might cause more sniggering in Sal's post-mortem with the organisers.

But what the hell! Leigh was very attractive and . . . what the hell?

The bar was empty, except for a lethargic young man who hadn't been expecting anyone until the proceedings in the dining room had finished, but still served them with reasonably good grace. Leigh opted for a malt whisky and Bill went along with the same.

'So why is the real Bill Stratton boring?' she asked, once they were ensconced in a plushly upholstered alcove.

'Well, I'm just . . . you heard what the guy who introduced me said. I've had a fairly easy ride in career terms — and in a career that has a disproportionately high public profile — but that doesn't make me interesting.'

'The guy who introduced you just chronicled the list of television companies who'd employed you and the different times at which you had read the news.'

'What's wrong with that? There's nothing more to say.'

'He didn't say anything about the *kind* of person you are.'

'That's not his job. No one here's interested in that stuff.'

'I am.'

'Oh.'

'So come on then . . . let's get the basics. Are you married?'

'Divorced.'

'How long ago?'

'Coming up for a year.'

'Children?'

'No.'

'On good terms with ex-wife?'

'Not adversarial. Hardly ever see her. She remarried.'

'Was her new husband the cause of the break-up?'

'Yes, I suppose he was. Though, from what Andrea says about the situation . . .' No, no, no need to confide that stuff. Not important. 'Actually, there was a very good "by way of contrast" line about a divorced woman in Caracas who —'

'I don't want to hear any more of those "by way of contrast" lines. I want to hear about you.'

And she did. To his amazement, Bill found himself telling her more than he'd told almost anyone. Andrea obviously knew greater detail, but she had received the information in a trickle effect through many years of marriage. He had never talked about himself for such a sustained period. He kept trying to divert the conversation on to Leigh and her life. He reciprocated her questions about marriages, divorces and children, but the answers didn't come. Leigh wasn't deliberately evasive; she just always asked for some other detail about his life that he couldn't resist responding to.

The Auction of Promises and subsequent money-sponging events came to an end, and the other guests drifted through into the bar, but Bill was hardly aware of them. He was caught up in Leigh's interrogation and in the translucent beam of her pale blue eyes.

At one point, a rather anxious-looking Keith/Derek/Alan broke into the aura of their conversation. 'Leigh, I was thinking maybe it was time to be going —'

'Fine.'

She gave no signs of moving. Keith/Derek/Alan stood loitering like a man outside a sex shop. 'Well, erm ...' he said after a time. 'Are you coming with me?'

'No.' It wasn't said with any edge or vindictiveness, just as a statement of fact.

'Ah.' The idea took a while to percolate

through into Keith/Derek/Alan's under-standing. 'Right. Well, I'll be off then.' He made two bold steps towards the door, then reassumed his loitering posture. 'So I'll call you, shall I?'

'Wouldn't bother.'

Though this was spoken as charmingly as Leigh's previous response, this time Keith/Derek/Alan was quicker to get the message. With a vainglorious 'Cheerio then', he strode off through the bar.

'A long-term relationship?' asked Bill.

'Couple of months. Never going to go the distance. He was boring. Should have recognised it earlier. Not enough time left to waste on non-starters.'

'How do you recognise a "non-starter"?' He was fishing, trying to gauge her reaction to him.

'That's the problem. When you start out, you don't know they're going to be non-starters . . . otherwise you wouldn't have started out, would you?'

He nodded, assimilating the logic of her words. 'So have you ever met anyone who wasn't a non-starter?'

'Given the fact that I am unmarried and not currently in a long-term relationship, the answer has to be no.'

That was more information than she'd

given him all evening. Not currently in a long-term relationship. But maybe, five minutes before, she had been in a long-term relationship with Keith/Derek/Alan? Did two months count as long-term?

'But presumably you're still looking for Mr. Right?'

'Mr Right was a concept I grew out of in my teens. The most I aspire to is Mr Right For The Time Being. And what I usually end up with is Mr Right For This Brief Moment . . . shortly to be re-identified as Mr Totally And Utterly Wrong.'

'Ah.'

'Still, one of the very few benefits I've found in getting old is that I have lowered expectations and I'm quicker to cut and run. If something doesn't work, I no longer feel any obligation to hang around and make it work. And I wish a lot of women had caught on to that idea a good deal earlier in their lives. I wish I had, come to that. God, the time I've wasted trying to turn men into something for which they never had the basic aptitude. But now I recognise the great truth, summed up by some country and western singer: "Shoes don't stretch and men don't change." '

'Does that mean you're anti-men, Leigh?'

'No, I still like them. I just don't expect much of them. That way, I am less often disappointed.'

'But you still go out with men?'

'Oh yes. But if there's no empathy there . . . or if the sex isn't any good . . . then I only do it the once.'

'Just like a man.'

'Yeah. Just like a man.'

The crowd of guests, their wallets emptied by an evening of charity, was beginning to thin. A few glanced towards the cocooned couple in the alcove. More sniggering to Sal on the phone, Bill thought mildly. Still, let's hope we can give them something to snigger about.

'They'll be closing the bar soon,' he said casually. 'Maybe we should continue our conversation up in my room?'

The pale blue eyes looked at him sceptically. 'So that you can make a clumsy pass at me?'

'No, no, I promise. I don't make clumsy passes. If we were both up in the bedroom . . . and if we discussed sex . . . and if we agreed we both wanted to . . . well . . .' He shrugged, in a manner that he hoped was eloquent.

'Hmm,' she said, after a silence. 'That sounds like a reasonably good system.'

'Well, it makes things kind of mutual, doesn't it?'

'Yes.'

'Consensual.'

'What a good word that is, Bill. Life-saver for men, isn't it? Makes them feel better about coming on to women.'

'I don't *come on* to women.'

'No? What've you been doing tonight?'

'We've been talking.'

'Mmm.' She nodded thoughtfully. 'Well, look, let's have the sex-or-no-sex discussion right here, rather than going up to your room.'

'Fine by me. Well, I do find you very attractive —'

She smiled, and looked at him. 'You're not without your attractions either.'

'We're both grown-up people —'

'And how. Neither of us will see sixty again.'

'So . . . ?'

'So. . . .' There was a very long silence. Bill was aware of the clatter of glasses being tidied up. 'So . . . no. We don't go and make love tonight.'

'Oh.' He wanted to ask why, but didn't.

'But . . . if you want to meet again. . . .' She handed him a card. 'There's my number.'

Then Leigh leant across, kissed his cheek and, before Bill had time to reciprocate, was on her way across the bar to the exit, in a glimmering of dark green.

This was different. Bill recognised the change. If he rang Leigh, he would be entering the arena of 'dating'. The other women he'd picked up on his after-dinner speaking jaunts had not been 'dates' — they'd been the products of opportunism. But, by refusing the invitation up to his room, Leigh had immediately put herself into a different scenario. And Bill was not sure that it was a scenario of which he wished to be part.

Asking someone out for a 'date' involved forward planning. The datee had to be contacted and, if she was agreeable, a mutually acceptable day and rendezvous then had to be arrived at. All of this seemed to Bill a rather stressful amount of organisation. To his surprise, the prospect also made him feel rather nervous. So many years had elapsed since he had last 'asked someone out' that he had forgotten the volatile panics that attended such bold gestures. In a hotel bar, emboldened by alcohol and isolation, he could be glibly confident, but the formal business of picking up a phone and asking

Leigh to 'go out with him' took him straight back to the jitteriness of adolescence.

Also, 'going on a date' did seem terribly public. In the varied groups of businessmen, sportsmen and charity supporters amongst whom he usually strutted his after-dinner speaking stuff, there was never anyone he knew. And, although the organisers might snigger to Sal about the women he went off with, she didn't know any of the individuals involved. But if he invited Leigh out, it would have to be to a decent restaurant, where he might well be seen by someone he knew. And the news would soon get around. Bill Stratton would be seen to be dating again for the first time since his divorce. This fact, for some reason, made him feel under a lot of pressure. He wasn't really worried about the press — by now he was too far down the alphabet of lists to be of much interest to them. Unless, of course, Leigh were famous in her own right . . .

He realised, with a little shock, that he had no idea whether she was or not. In fact, he knew nothing about her, just about her attitude to men. But he did want to know more. The deeper worry he had about 'going out with someone' was the fear of being defined by the person he was with. He remembered the feeling from the very early stage of his relationship with Andrea. Most of the time they had got on fine, but he recalled occasions when she had annoyed him — particularly by something she said in company — and he had wanted to disown her. He had wanted to say, No, she's not with me. I have an identity that is separate from hers. I'm not like she is. The feeling was one which, as they settled into the routine of marriage, soon dissipated, and he had completely forgotten about it until the prospect came of his being seen in public with a woman again. (Strangely, no such worries assailed him when he was with Ginnie or Sal or Carolyn. But then he'd known them and often been seen out with them while he was still married. The divorce hadn't changed anything so far as those three relationships were concerned . . . or at least the public perception was that nothing had changed so far as those three relationships were concerned.)

He did find he was thinking a lot about Leigh, though. He wouldn't have dignified his feelings with the description of 'love', but he was certainly interested. He wondered for a moment whether that was simply because she had said no to him. Though not a great expert on the psychological advice doled out in women's magazines, he did know about the recommended principle of 'playing hard to get'. Saying no to a man was supposed to be the sure-fire way to stimulate his interest.

But other women had said no to Bill. He had gone down his after-dinner conversation route a good few times without a result. When the suggestion of adjourning up to his hotel room had arisen, there had been some who'd turned down the rich gift on offer. And, except for a mild immediate tug of frustration, he had felt and thought little more about them. But he did keep thinking about Leigh. He was going to have to ring her.

'Erm, hello, it's Bill Stratton . . .'
'Yes?'
He'd expected more; some hesitation in recognising him, possibly even some enthusiasm at recognising him.
'Is that Leigh?'
'Of course it is. Otherwise I wouldn't have known who you are, would I? Unless, of course, you'd rung the number of one of your other girlfriends by mistake.'
One of your other girlfriends? Surely she didn't know Sal, or hadn't logged on to 'billstrattonssexualencounters.com', had

she? But he was being paranoid.

'No, no. Well, I'm glad it's you. And I'm Bill Stratton.'

'I think we've established that.'

'We met at that charity do at —'

'Bill, I may be over sixty, but I'm glad to say the Alzheimer's hasn't kicked in yet. I do remember the occasion.'

'Yes, well, we did, erm . . . talk about possibly meeting up again . . .'

'I remember that too.'

'Good.' Having successfully negotiated the conversation so far, Bill felt he needed a little breather, so took one.

When she thought she had waited quite long enough, Leigh asked, with some exasperation. 'So, do you think it's a good idea? Or have you taken the trouble to ring me to tell me you think it's a bad idea?'

'No, no. I think it's a very good idea. I just wondered if you did too . . . think it's a good idea, that is . . . ?'

'Yes, fine,' she said airily.

'So you would like to come out with me?'

'Sure.'

'Good.' That significant point having been achieved, he felt in need of another breather.

'On the other hand,' she said after a while, 'it would be easier for me to sort out the logistics if you actually had a date in mind.'

'Yes, yes, of course.' He suggested the following Friday. She couldn't do it. The Saturday. She could. He mentioned a restaurant which was swish enough to show he was making an effort, but not one of his regular haunts. There was only a minimal chance of his being spotted there.

'So . . .' he wound up slowly, 'I'll look forward to seeing you then.'

'So will I. Bye.'

And the line went dead.

Bill didn't know exactly what he felt after that. Was he being hypersensitive, or had Leigh sounded a bit low-key? Businesslike perhaps, rather than warm? What did she actually think of him? Did she think anything of him at all? What was going on inside her head?

For the first time in a long period of negative thoughts on the subject, he became aware that his early marriage to Andrea had had benefits too. At least it had saved him from the endless second guessing involved in the dating game.

Chapter fifteen

. . . and, by way of contrast, in a Galashiels hospital there is a notice on the door of one of the male wards which reads: 'Afternoon Visiting — Wives Only — One per Patient.'

The restaurant had been a good choice. Excellent food, low lighting, discreet service, and not a face Bill had ever seen before in his life. Leigh was looking good, in a linen suit the colour of wholemeal bread.

She once again dictated the direction of the conversation. Bill hadn't realised before quite how strong her personality was. But that strength didn't deter him. Leigh was just direct and, by implication, honest. And she wouldn't let him take the easy option of wheeling out his 'by way of contrast' lines. Again, she wanted to find out about him.

And again, Bill was surprised by how much he let his defences drop in what he told her. By the end of the evening she knew all about his marriage to Andrea and its demise. She knew about Dewi and his ready-made family. She even knew quite a lot about Bill's relationship with his parents and his reactions to their deaths.

But he, frustratingly, still knew very little about her. There was an ex-husband in the background and, he managed to infer from things she said, two children somewhere. But details like their names, their professions, or how Leigh felt about them were not offered. Nor, though there was an implication that it might be something in the world of psychiatry, did he get a precise definition of the kind of work she had done . . . or indeed whether she still did it. Somehow, each time, at the point when Bill should have asked a supplementary question, the conversation had moved on.

The reason the conversation moved on was that Leigh always got in her supplementary question first and Bill, who hadn't had much experience of it recently, found he rather enjoyed talking about himself. He was conscious on some level that Leigh was doing what he had done in all of his recent sexual encounters — maintaining personal privacy by expressing a lot of interest in the other person — but he was quite enjoying her interrogation. A pleasant change to meet someone new who was actually interested in him.

And there was something to be said for actual dating, rather than shuffling anonymous women off to anonymous hotel rooms. He was surprised how nervous he had been all day about the prospect of meeting Leigh that first evening. His anxiety had made him pee a lot, and peeing a lot had made him anxious about whether he'd got a prostate problem. But once he was actually with her, the worries melted away.

Until ordering coffee heralded the end of the evening. Then he started to get nervous again. He couldn't forget Leigh's strictures about the men she went out with. 'But if there's no empathy there . . . or if the sex isn't any good . . . then I only do it the once.' To him there seemed to have been empathy during their evening together, but he didn't know whether it had come up to her standards. And if he had passed the empathy test, whether he'd come up to her standards sexually? Once again he was made aware of the perils of dating, of not knowing what the other person was thinking, of not knowing how to bring up the subject of what the other person was thinking.

Leigh's typical directness dealt with his second anxiety. 'We seem to get on all right, don't we . . . at least so far as talking's concerned . . .'

Bill agreed that indeed they did.

'So, shall we see whether the sex works too?'

As she said this, she put her hand on his, and tickled along the top of it with her middle finger.

'Well, that would be . . . very nice.' He knew it sounded feeble as he said it.

'Right. Two rules. We go back to my place. And when I ask you to, you leave. Happy with that?'

Bill agreed that he was indeed happy with that.

Leigh had a small house in Clerkenwell. A whole house, but there was no evidence of anyone else living there. No photos on the mantelpiece to open windows onto the rest of her life, though a collection of books on psychology reinforced the impression Bill had received of the kind of work she did. The décor of the house was affluent without being flamboyant.

As she gave him a drink in the sitting room, Leigh said, 'Another ground rule: no love.'

'How do you mean?'

'We're going to go to bed together, because we like each other and we think the sex might be enjoyable. But neither of us need pretend that there's anything more than friendship involved. No clingy emotions, all right?'

'Fine.' They were the words men had been wanting to hear from women since Eve refused to say them to Adam.

'Okay.' She gulped down the remains of her wine. 'Let's see how we go.'

They went pretty well. Leigh knew what she was doing, and she knew what she wanted. Bill, after his long schooling by Andrea, knew what he was doing and could supply what she wanted.

'Good,' Leigh sighed, after an hour of other contented sighings.

'Do I pass the test?' asked Bill. 'Or wasn't the sex any good?' He wouldn't have asked if her body hadn't already given him the answer.

'No, very nice. Thank you.'

'Thank *you*. So, Leigh, we could do it again?'

She sat up in bed and shrugged. 'Could happen. No reason why it shouldn't from a purely qualitative perspective.'

'Then from what perspective might it not happen?'

'Bill, there are so many reasons why things don't happen. Let's just not go into them.'

'Okay.'

She rolled over and consulted her watch. He looked with pleasure at the firmness of her back. Yes, the skin was a little more crepey than it once had been. But still beautiful.

'I need to sleep, Bill. You'd better go.'

A bit abrupt, but not too hurtful. He might have worried if she hadn't so patently enjoyed the last hour.

He kissed her gently on the nose, got up and started to dress.

Leigh luxuriated in the space of her bed. 'One of the great benefits of no longer being married is no longer feeling I should share a bed with someone. I sleep so much better. Have you found that?'

'Well . . .' He hadn't thought about the question before. 'Yes, I think I probably have.'

'Beds are wonderful for making love in, but sleeping together . . . who needs it?'

'A lot of your attitudes are very masculine, Leigh.'

'Yes, they are. A few years ago, I did a kind of overview of relationships, a cold hard look, and I asked myself which gender did better out of them. There was no question, men had it easier. So I thought I'd take a few leaves out of their book.'

'And has it worked?'

'Certainly has. I've learnt the skill of compartmentalising my life.'

'And sex has a compartment all its own, does it?'

She gave him a foxy grin which was at odds with the innocence of her clear blue eyes. 'At least one.'

He was dressed. 'So shall I ring you?'

'Do that.'

As a late cab drove him back to Pimlico, Bill played the evening back in his mind. Pretty good, he thought. He'd rather have got in the 'Well, I'd better be on my way' before Leigh had done the 'You'd better go', but that was a small negative in what had been a generally very positive experience.

He decided he wouldn't do the customary Interflora order the next morning. He'd ring her instead. This one he wanted to continue.

And it did continue. The pattern had been set. They never planned their next meeting as they parted from the last one. Bill would ring Leigh the following morning and they would fix a date for their next encounter. Her diary was full and unpredictable, his was cluttered with after-dinner speaking bookings, but they managed to meet every ten days or so.

The pattern set by the first evening was also maintained. A good dinner somewhere off Bill's beaten track, which he paid for, then a return to Clerkenwell for an hour of good sex. And, though he did finally establish that she worked as a psychotherapist, Leigh still found out more about him than he did about her. But that didn't worry him. He respected — and sympathised with — her need to compartmentalise her life.

Time passed. Bill realised with a shock that he had been 'dating' Leigh for three months. He found he was increasingly looking forward to their meetings. Having someone in his life was a good feeling. Soon he might consider introducing her to some of his friends. Trevor for sure. The former director's depressed ramblings in The Annexe had got so boring that Bill needed something to liven their sessions up. Leigh might be just the thing.

Then Ginnie . . . well, Ginnie was still away in Croatia playing nuns with dirty habits. And when he thought about it, for some reason he didn't really want to introduce Leigh to the actress. His relationship with Ginnie was obviously platonic, but it was an exclusive one, nonetheless. They worked best on a one-to-one basis.

Carolyn . . . well, Leigh had expressed so little interest in — indeed, had been so positively bored by the whole BWOC concept — that maybe that was another introduction that could wait.

But Sal . . . yes, he'd like to introduce his agent to his new . . . what was the word? Girlfriend? Yuk. Mistress, maybe . . . except could a man without a wife actually have a mistress? Well, introduce his agent to Leigh, anyway. The sexual *frisson* he'd felt when he told Sal he loved her had been rather forgotten in the flurry of real sex with Leigh. And it would be quite fun to surprise Sal with the news that there was another ongoing woman in his life.

But he didn't get the chance to surprise her. His agent — perhaps predictably — already knew about Leigh.

'But how on earth . . . ?'

'Another of my clients recognised you in a restaurant, with the same woman — twice.'

'Ah. And he didn't snigger as he told you?'

'No. No sniggering. He said she was a very pretty lady.'

'She certainly is, Sal.'

'And you're seeing her regularly?'

'On and off.'

'But more on than off?'

'I suppose so.'

'So are you going to introduce me? Do I get to meet her?'

'It's funny. I was just thinking . . . it'd be nice if you did.'

'Bill, you're maturing.'

'What do you mean by that?'

'You've stopped picking up women you're ashamed of. Now you've got one you want to show off.'

'Well, yes, maybe I have, in a way.'

The more he thought about it, the more functions he could imagine attending with Leigh. He wouldn't drag her out on after-dinner speaking dates, but there were plenty of receptions and launches he got invited to where it would be nice to have an attractive woman on his arm.

Yes, it was about time his relationship with Leigh became a bit more public.

Leigh herself, however, proved to be remarkably unkeen on the idea. 'Bill, I'm of the "if it ain't broke, don't fix it" school. What we have works well. We both enjoy it, and we have no "external factors" to spoil anything. From my experience of marriage, most start out with the couple themselves getting on okay. It's the pressure of other people that drives them apart. Other people, in the form of fathers and mothers — particularly mothers — children, friends who one partner likes better than the other partner does. That's what drives wedges between lovers — other people. What we have, Bill, is very good, but it'll only stay very good if we keep it —'

'Compartmentalised?'

'That was the very word I was prompting you to utter.'

'Right.' Bill found it odd. With all his other sexual encounters, the last thing he'd wanted was to introduce the woman to any of his friends. Now Leigh had denied him that option, he wanted more and more to parade her as his, to get her to meet some of his friends. Sal, if nobody else.

'But do you think, in time, our relationship will develop so that we do want to be a bit more generally sociable?'

'Who knows, Bill? Like I say, "if it ain't broke . . ." '

Chapter sixteen

. . . and, by way of contrast, a member of the Australian Parliament, exposed by the tabloid press for maintaining seven mistresses, has just been appointed Minister for Employment.

'So I gather you have a new girlfriend.'

'What? How do you . . . ? Sal?'

Carolyn nodded. Bill wasn't sure how he felt about her knowing. But he should have anticipated it. Forget the imaginary 'billstrattonssexualencounters.com' website — that wasn't needed as long as Sal was around. And Sal and Carolyn were regularly in touch about BWOC business, so . . .

'Nice, is she?'

'Yes. Yes, very nice.'

'Good. Anything like Andrea?'

'No. No, I don't think so.' This was the first time he'd thought about the question. Leigh certainly didn't maunder on about the NHS, and she wasn't vegetarian. But whether she'd consider going on holiday to a nice hotel in a nice resort as being in 'a tourist trap' . . . he didn't know. In fact, it struck him, he didn't really know a great deal about Leigh.

Nor, when he came to make the comparison, did he remember a great deal about Andrea. It was amazing how a body of information built up over more than three decades had eroded away to leave only the vaguest vestiges of memory.

'Because, in my experience,' Carolyn went on, 'after a divorce — however messy — a lot of men go back to the same type of women.'

'Like dogs returning to their vomit?'

'You always did have a way with words, Bill.'

'Hmm. Well, I'm pretty confident that Leigh has absolutely nothing in common with Andrea — except for the number of legs.'

'And breasts, presumably?'

Since she'd brought the subject up, he couldn't help admiring the comforting curves of Carolyn's bosom. Her nipples looked hard and prominent . . . what was that expression he'd heard from some raucous male friend . . . ? Her headlights were on, yes.

Again he came back to the eternal question — why do men think about sex all the time? Surely by the age of sixty that knee-jerk reaction should have trickled away to nothingness. But it hadn't. He found himself idly wondering what Carolyn would look like naked.

'So, will I be meeting her? Leigh, was it?'

'That's her name, yes.'

'But you won't be bringing her into the office?'

'Doesn't feature in my current plans, no. Just a very casual relationship at this point. We enjoy each other's company —'

'Company?' The brazen look in her eye managed to encompass all the innuendoes that could be contained in that innocent word.

'Yes.'

'Well, I'm glad you've got someone,' she said, totally matter-of-fact. 'Means I don't have to worry about you mooching around alone round your flat in Pimlico.'

'Did you worry about that?'

But Carolyn wasn't the sort to bite at such blatant emotional fishing. 'Worry? God, no. Incidentally, Jason wants to set up some more links on the website. It'll cost a bit.'

'Sounds all right.'

'Yeah. As his Mum, I feel slightly guilty asking, because I know how much he needs the money. Setting up as a stand-up comic and writer wasn't the greatest career move he ever made. But I don't think he's having us on. The website does need to keep being developed and —'

'Carolyn, you know I trust you implicitly. And I trust Jason too. I'll agree to anything you want me to do.'

She was a woman who could never resist a double entendre. 'Really, Bill? When was the last time I had an offer like that?'

'Had a call from one of the ex-wives today.'

'Oh yes? Which one?'

'Doesn't matter. She'd got a bloody nerve, though.'

'Asking for money, was she?'

'No, not this time. It was something else.'

They were sitting, predictably enough, in The Annexe. A televised football match meant the pub was full, collectively sighing, moaning and shouting to the rhythms of the game. Bill and Trevor had pints in front of them. Even more indulgent, each had a packet of pork scratchings. An archetypal masculine nirvana . . . except that, try as he might, Bill had never managed to find football interesting. Still, the pint and the pork scratchings gave him a sufficient sense of machismo.

He waited, letting Trevor time his own narration.

'The bitch wants me to go out with her.'

'What? Rekindle the flames of passion?'

'God, no. She's just got this work gig where, as she put it, "I'd look better with a man with me." And then she did all this . . . surely we've known each other long enough, and the divorce is long enough ago for us to be civil to each other . . . we're grown-ups . . . I'm sure in the same situation, I'd be happy to help you out . . . Go on, for old times' sake . . .'

'So, for old times' sake, did you agree?'

'Did I hell?! I know what she wants to do. She wants to impress whoever it is at this work thing with how mature she is. What a modern, sensible woman, having such a good relationship with her ex-husband that they can spend the odd evening together, with no embarrassment or recrimination. What she bloody forgets is that our entire marriage was nothing but embarrassment and recrimination. When we split up, we loathed each other. No, I'm sorry, when she asked me, I told her — stuff that for a game of soldiers.'

'So do you still loathe each other?'

'That, Bill, is not the point.' There was a collective howl of frustration from the pub as an open goal was missed. Trevor waited for the noise to subside before continuing.

'It's about my self-image.'

'I didn't know you had a self-image.'

'Well, I do. And it's not one I want let down by being seen in the company of that bitch.'

'Ah.'

'That's the trouble . . . as a man, you're judged by the woman you're with. On my own, I'm fine. I don't know what people think of me —'

'They probably see you as a bitter, disappointed, impotent alcoholic.'

'They probably do. And that's all right. I can live with that. It may not be a particularly attractive image, but at least it's mine. What they see is what they get. Whereas if I turn up to this gig with the ex-wife, what kind of image of me does that project?'

'Well —'

'I'll tell you. It makes me look like the kind of wimp who's so mature and broad-minded and grown-up that I can have an enjoyable evening with my ex-wife. Well, bloody hell, I don't want people to think that of me.'

'No, I suppose I can see your point.'

'When you're on your own, Bill, you have control over the image you present. Minute you're seen out with a woman, that's what you're judged by.'

'Yes, but some people make that into an advantage. Why do all these older men marry trophy wives? Why does every man want to be seen with a supermodel on his arm?'

Bill tried to assess whether he had ever been guilty of such an ambition. And he decided that, amongst the many things he could have been accused of, that wasn't one.

'Well,' said Trevor, 'maybe it works for some of them. All I'd say is think hard before you're seen in public with a woman.'Cause it's the woman people will judge you by.'

There was a silence. Bill assimilated what his friend had said. Yes, there was something in it. Maybe he shouldn't rush into displaying Leigh in public. Maybe she should stay under wraps for a little longer. Keep his options open.

He took a long contemplative swig of beer, and bit down hard on a pork scratching. He heard a cracking sound, and felt a strange sensation on his tongue.

This time there was a goal. The pub erupted. In the chaos of masculine ecstasy, Bill spat out the contents of his mouth.

In the palm of his hand lay the intact pork scratching, and half a yellowed tooth.

The next day he was glad he had made the decision to maintain as much secrecy as possible about Leigh, because he had a call from Ginnie. One of her co-stars, playing a precociously sexually-aware novice, had developed shingles. Though the producers had tried to organise a rewrite to transform the whole convent into a veiled order of nuns, it hadn't worked. Nor had the proposal to introduce an epidemic of Black Death to justify the spots, so shooting had been rescheduled to get other stuff in the can until the actress's face cleared up. Since the bulk of the novice's scenes were with her Mother Superior, Virginia Fairbrother also had an unexpected break.

Was 'one of our dinners' possible? Bill said it certainly was.

The restaurant this time had the trendily ambiguous name of Cruising. The theme, obviously enough, was Thirties cruise ship, even to the point of having false portholes set into the walls. It was a huge space with lots of sweeping staircases and mahogany railings. There was a large dance floor and a live band playing such classics as 'Nice Work If You Can Get It', 'Basin Street Blues' and 'Cocktails for Two'. Inevitably, the place was a 'concept restaurant' which encouraged clients to 'dress up and make an evening of it.' People who wanted to sit at the Captain's Table had to wear full evening dress. Converting the premises had cost millions and, since its opening two weeks before, the restaurant had been wildly popular. Bookings for names that weren't on special lists could be months away.

But the wrinkle on Ginnie's fine nose suggested she didn't think the good times would last.

'Trouble is, a place like this costs so much just to keep running. And to generate any atmosphere, it has to be full. Once the bookings start to drop off, the whole enterprise will go bottom up very quickly.'

'Like the Titanic . . .'

'Which it rather spookily resembles. Yes, Bill.'

The name of Virginia Fairbrother had instantly secured their table. And the cocktails really were good. She looked wonderful again, this time in a minimal black halter-necked dress that showed acres of her smoothly tanned skin. God, this is nice, thought Bill. Sitting at a restaurant table opposite a beautiful woman. I could happily spend my life doing that. Then the thought occurred to him that he actually *did* spend a lot of his life doing that.

Still, seeing Ginnie was doing him a power of good. He had had one of his rare down moments after leaving The Annexe. Trevor's gloom hadn't infected him — he was inured to that — but the broken tooth had. The accident seemed symbolic, a reminder that his body would not last for ever, a little dental *memento mori*. He could still feel the unexpectedly rough edge against his tongue, but it didn't worry him now. Not when he'd got Ginnie to look at.

The hazel eyes shrewdly took him in over the frosted rim of her cocktail glass. 'So . . . are you still working your wicked way through the desperate and grateful older women of Britain?'

He had known the question would come up. The vehemence of her denunciation at their last meeting had shocked him. And what she'd said then had made him change his behaviour. He had wanted to save up telling her that, like an unexpected present hidden away in a pocket, but he wasn't going to get a better cue than the one she had just given him.

'Actually, Ginnie,' he said, serious for once, 'I did think a lot about what you said to me —'

'I'm honoured.'

'No, you were right. I was just using

women. All those anonymous pick-ups in anonymous hotels . . . there was something slightly sordid about it.'

'I'm glad you recognise that.'

'The phrase of yours I couldn't get out of my mind was "passionless promiscuity".'

'Honoured to have made an impression.'

'So, anyway, I have, sort of . . . well, it sounds like something out of a social worker's report, but I have "changed my behaviour".'

'Goodness, the effect a woman's words can have.'

'Not any woman's words, Ginnie.'

His eyes met hers. There was a moment of stillness between them.

'So . . . all these desperate and grateful older women are still desperate, but have no cause to be grateful?'

'Well, you could put it like that.'

'Haven't you been tempted, though?'

'Yes. Yes, I have.' He recounted the non-encounter in Nottingham. 'And I didn't do anything,' he concluded with some smugness.

'Good. Well done. So having rediscovered your libido, you've now put it firmly under wraps again, have you?'

'Well . . .' Bill couldn't really see anything to be gained by telling Ginnie about Leigh.

It would only confuse the issue. And it might very probably break the current atmosphere of complicity at their table. The longer he spent with Ginnie, the more he enjoyed the experience. He felt glad he hadn't gone down the road of making Leigh a more public part of his life.

'I've decided,' he said piously, 'to do what you suggested.'

'Which bit of what I suggested?'

'The bit about waiting till I feel something for someone before I go to bed with them.'

Ginnie cocked a sardonic eye at him. 'Really? Well, I must pat myself on the back, I think. I'd never before seen myself as a sentimental educationalist, but I seem to have succeeded at my first attempt. I've made you give up your wicked ways. I've made you realize what an arid experience sex can be, when it doesn't come with *lurve* attached.'

She was laying on the irony, but he knew there was an underlying truth in what she said. Part of him wanted to tell her that he'd progressed even further than that, that he was currently enjoying sex with a woman for whom he was beginning to have quite strong feelings. But the other part of him fortunately realised that such confidences might be better unshared.

With the lightning speed that her profession had refined in her, Ginnie's manner changed from mocking to intimate. 'Love often arises where you least expect it,' she breathed. 'I mean, the *coup de foudre* is wonderful — seeing someone for the first time across a room and just feeling this huge surge of necessity, the knowledge that you want to be with them. But it's not the only way. Increasingly I'm coming round to the view that the other kind is better.'

'What other kind?'

'The love that grows slowly. The person you've known forever, whom you suddenly see with new eyes. I have a director friend,' she murmured, 'who maintains that there is no relationship between a man and a woman that does not have a sexual element, that if you find you go on wanting to see a member of the opposite sex, then there's going to be an element of fancying there.'

'Mmm.' Bill looked deep into the famous eyes. 'Well, I've never pretended that I don't fancy you.' Then, feeling this might be too direct, he lightened his declaration by adding, 'But then every man in the country fancies you.'

Ginnie's voice was even throatier as she said, 'There's a big difference between being admired as an abstract image, and being admired for oneself, as a real woman.'

He didn't trust himself with anything more than another 'Mmm.'

She leant across the table and laid her hand gently on top of his. The band was playing "I've Got My Love To Keep Me Warm", and Bill was thinking boldly that they might have a dance after dinner.

It must have been the movement of Ginnie's hand that made him look suddenly across the room. Up until then he'd been cocooned, hermetically sealed in the force field between their eyes. But as Ginnie put her hand on his, Bill's peripheral vision glimpsed a matching gesture at another table.

He looked across. On the other side of the dance floor, like a mirror image, another man and woman sat at a table. The woman had just placed her hand over the man's, and was tickling along the top of it with her middle finger.

The man he'd never seen before in his life. But the woman was Leigh.

The man — who, Bill noticed with some chagrin, was a good fifteen years younger than him — laughed in response to her tickling. He rose and, taking her by the hand, led Leigh out of the restaurant. As they left the room, he put his arm around her waist in a way that contrived to be both comforting and intimate.

Bill looked back, open-mouthed, to find Ginnie's hazel eyes fixed curiously on him. Both her hands were back on her lap. 'Someone you know?'

'I thought it was, but, er, no . . . I must have made a mistake.'

The evening was ruined. Whatever intimacy had built up between them quickly seeped away. They talked in generalities. Ginnie entertained Bill with stories of hilarious doings on the set of her Sister Saga, and he even found himself quoting 'by way of contrast' lines at her. Their conversation was bright and brittle, they laughed a lot and at the end of the evening, they didn't dance.

By the time he got back to his Pimlico flat, Bill Stratton was feeling wretched. The broken tooth ached, and his mood was not improved by a message on the answering machine. He immediately recognised the irritating prissy Welshness of Dewi's voice.

'Bill, Andrea wanted me to let you know that she's in hospital.'

Chapter seventeen

. . . and, by way of contrast, a member of a French swimming team was too embarrassed to turn up for a regional competition because he had been experimenting with Viagra the night before.

Bill rang through to Dewi's surgery the following morning. The receptionist said Dr Roberts would be with patients until about eleven, but she would pass on the message.

It was nearly half-past twelve when the call came. While he waited, Bill was uncharacteristically twitchy. He wasn't really worried about Andrea, though her hospitalisation added another layer of unease to his feelings. Mostly, his discomfort sprang from what had happened the night before. He felt doubly unfortunate. The growing closeness of his relationship with Ginnie had been put into reverse, and God only knew where he stood with Leigh. He thought of ringing her, but he didn't want to risk missing Dewi's call back. Also he wasn't quite sure what he would say if he did get through to her.

His mood wasn't improved by the fact

that he had a dull, dry hangover. Over-compensating for the diminishing sense of intimacy with Ginnie, he had ordered one bottle too many, and drunk most of it himself. The face that had bleared out of his shaving mirror at him that morning, with its white fuzz of bristles, had been that of an old man.

On top of that, the broken tooth was really hurting now. He'd have to make an appointment with his dentist, a procedure he never particularly relished. At one stage of the morning, he picked up the phone to do the deed, but replaced it quickly, still worried about missing Dewi.

When the call finally came, Bill's ex-wife's husband made no pretence of wanting to talk to him. 'I'm only calling because Andrea insisted. She said you ought to know.'

'Well, yes, if she's in hospital, I'd want to know.' But was that true? He'd thought so little about Andrea in the eighteen months since the divorce that perhaps the details of her life really were of no interest to him. 'So what's she done? Broken something?' He hoped the tone of his enquiry contained the right mix of lightness and concern.

'No, it's rather more serious than that.' Dewi's voice was full of righteous reproof.

No doubt Andrea had talked to him at great length about her ex-husband's 'shallowness'. Bill Stratton couldn't be expected even to take serious things seriously.

'What is it then?'

'Andrea has cancer.'

'God.' He felt winded by the answer, and struggled for his words. 'What, but I mean . . . where?'

'The lungs.'

'Lungs. But Andrea never smoked.'

'Lung cancer is not always smoking-related.' It was the medical man's rebuke to the non-specialist.

'But . . . I mean . . . how bad is it?'

'Bad enough.' Dewi managed almost to sound smug as he said the words. 'She's had a course of chemotherapy which it's hoped has reduced the tumour. She's in hospital at the moment for some tests to see whether they're going to have to operate.'

'Oh, God. But when . . . ? How long ago was it diagnosed?'

'Four months.'

'Why on earth didn't anyone tell me before?'

'There was a general view . . .' said Dewi, building up an image of Bill being discussed at Roberts' family councils, 'that you wouldn't be interested.'

'Of course I'd be interested. I was married to Andrea for nearly forty years.'

'Hmm.' There was a wealth of disapproval in the monosyllable.

'So . . . Dewi . . .' He managed to bring himself to use the name '. . . what's the prognosis?'

'Andrea's not my patient,' came the prim response.

'No, but you must have some idea.'

'Her future is very much dependent on the outcome of these tests. Depends how effective the chemo has been. We'll have to see what her consultant says.'

'But . . . how is she?' As soon as he said it, he knew it was a stupid question.

'Nobody tends to be at their best when they've got lung cancer.'

'I know that. Still, how is — ?'

'Well, of course Andrea's a wonderfully strong woman. She's being very brave, doing everything not to upset the children.'

Yes, of course, the Roberts brood would be involved too. 'But she's being looked after all right, is she?'

Dewi took that as a direct insult. 'I can assure you she is! She's having the best medical care available. I go and see her every day, and the children have worked out a rota of visiting. Andrea is in very good hands.'

'I'm sure she is, yes. I didn't mean to give the impression that —'

'Well, you did.'

'I'm sorry.'

'Now I do have a surgery to run, so —'

'Dewi . . .' The name didn't get any easier to say. 'Would it be possible for me to see Andrea?'

There was a sharp intake of breath from the other end of the line. 'I don't see why that should be necessary.'

'Please . . . I would like to see her.'

'She might not want to see you.'

'I agree, she might not. But would you ask her?'

The idea clearly didn't appeal. 'Bill, if I'd had my way, I wouldn't be speaking to you now. I'm only doing so because Andrea asked me to. That's what she wanted.'

'In just the same way, she might want to see me.'

'I doubt it.'

'Please. Will you ask her?'

'I'll discuss it with the children. See what they think.'

God, thought Bill as he put the phone down. Another bloody Roberts family council will be summoned to discuss more of my shortcomings.

He was shocked by the news of Andrea's

illness, but he felt so detached from her life that it hardly seemed real to him. On his shelf was a small medical dictionary which had somehow survived the dispersal of belongings from the Putney house. There was no specific entry for the lung variety, just a general piece on cancer. One sentence from the article stood out. 'Some cancers can be caused by physical factors; a broken tooth or badly fitting denture can give rise to a chronic mouth ulcer which does not heal and undergoes malignant change.'

He tried not to think about it. He made an appointment with his dentist and decided to find some undemanding company over lunch in the pub. Then, in an attempt to drive out thoughts of death by thoughts of continuing life, he rang Leigh. Yes, she'd like to meet. She was free that evening.

Neither of them mentioned being at Cruising the previous night.

There were a million reasons why it could have happened, but he had a feeling that the real one was the news about Andrea. But he couldn't tell Leigh that. She'd think he was just fishing for sympathy. Up until that point the evening had followed its usual pattern. A pleasant dinner in an obscure restaurant, idle conversation, and back to the house in Clerkenwell.

It was only when they got into bed that everything went wrong. Bill, like most men, had had occasional bouts of impotence during his marriage. General tiredness or excessive booze had from time to time taken their toll. Remarkably, though, during his sexual encounters in anonymous hotels since the divorce, the problem hadn't arisen . . . and fortunately something else had. But he'd never before encountered what happened that night in Leigh's bed.

Or rather what didn't happen.

Nothing.

The beauties of her body, the murmuring dirtiness of her voice, the urging of her hands and . . . nothing. Bill ransacked his memory for ever more obscene images to rouse him to some kind of action, but the transmission cable between brain and groin appeared to have been permanently severed. When it became finally clear that her efforts were having no effect, Leigh rolled away from him.

'I don't quite know . . .' Bill began hesitantly.

'It happens.' Her tone was even, not exactly unsympathetic, but hardly encouraging.

'I suppose I could try Viagra,' he suggested, in a way that he hoped sounded humorous.

'I don't care what you do, so long as it works . . .' She touched him lightly. 'Which this currently doesn't.'

'No.'

She turned her pale blue, Irish-looking eyes on him. 'Is this something to do with last night?'

'What?'

'Cruising. We were both there with other dates.'

'I didn't know you'd seen me.'

'Of course I did. You were only the other side of the dance floor.'

'Yes.'

'Well, is this something to do with that?'

'What do you mean?'

'Oh, God knows the way you men's minds work. But the fact that you saw me with someone else last night might . . . I don't know, bring on performance anxiety . . . make you jealous . . .'

Bill saw a potential way out that would leave him with some honour intact. 'Well, yes, as a matter of fact, I —'

Leigh raised a hand to silence him. 'I don't want to hear any of it. I'm not in this to mend your bruised ego or cure your feelings of inadequacy. That's what I do all day at work. In my social life I don't want to hear about people's complications.'

'But, Leigh . . .' He wasn't going to throw away the excuse she had offered him. 'It was quite a shock for me to see you with another man.'

'Why? Have we ever had an agreement that involves fidelity? Have we ever even discussed the subject? I don't ask you what you do with your life when you're not with me, and I think you should allow me the same freedom. Sauce for the goose or something of the sort.'

'Yes, that's fine, but just . . . well, seeing you with someone else . . .' He decided to try the sentimental escape route '. . . I suppose it made me realise how much you do mean to me.'

'Crap. What I mean to you is that I'm someone you have good sex with. It's like meeting someone with whom you have a good game of squash.'

'No more?' he asked, knowing he sounded pathetic.

'No. You've got a nerve, anyway. I don't know why you're getting at me. I have as much right to go out with who I want to as you do.'

'Yes, of course.'

'And I'm afraid I don't buy that gender

difference argument. You can behave like that because you're a man, whereas I'm a weak feeble sentimental woman —'

'I wasn't using that argument. I just . . . well, I thought we had something going between us.'

'We did. As I said, very enjoyable sex.'

He wanted to ask, Was that all? but couldn't bring himself to. There were limits to how feeble and feminine he could sound.

'And, incidentally, Bill, there is a bit of pot and kettle going on here. I would point out that when you saw me at Cruising with my date, you weren't alone yourself.'

'No, but . . . she's been a friend for ever. And also —'

'What?'

'I mean, that woman I was with . . .'

'Virginia Fairbrother,' she said dismissively. 'Yes, I did recognise her.'

'Well, I didn't go to bed with her.'

'I don't care whether you went to bed with her or not. It's not my business.'

'I never have been to bed with her.'

'Bill, I don't want to hear your life history.'

'Well, you've heard plenty of my life history. You kept asking me about myself.'

'Yes, but that was just for professional reasons.'

'Oh?'

'As a psychotherapist, I have to find out what makes people tick. It's an occupational hazard. But I've never wanted to get into a situation where I have to start treating you. Evenings I'm off duty. All I've ever wanted from you was good uncomplicated sex.'

He let out a dry chuckle. 'That's what *men* are supposed to say.'

'I thought you weren't going to use the gender argument.'

'No, I'm not . . . I just . . . I thought I meant something to you, Leigh.'

'You did. You had two things going for you. You were an amusing companion and a good lover. Now we seem to be reduced to one thing, and quite honestly, I can always find myself amusing companionship.'

'And other good lovers?'

Leigh smiled complacently. 'Oh yes.'

He felt the need to move the conversation on. 'Tonight, I mean . . . what happened . . . or didn't happen . . . I'm sure it's just a blip. I mean, I don't think I'm, like, impotent for life. It will come back . . . you know, with a bit of care and concentration and relaxation.'

'Bill, I'm not about to take on the role of a sex therapist. Just accept the facts. We had a nice time, we enjoyed each other's company, we enjoyed each other's bodies . . . and now that little interlude has come to an end.'

'So don't you want to meet again?'

'There doesn't seem to be a lot of point. We were going to finish soon, anyway.'

'Were we?'

'Yes. I'd been getting the feeling recently that we'd run our course. Hadn't you?'

'No.'

She shrugged. To her it seemed the whole affair was already in the past.

'So we just part, do we, Leigh? I go through that door, and we don't see each other again?'

'Sounds about right, yes.'

'We don't even talk on the phone?'

'What would be the point of that? What do we have to say to each other?'

'But . . . do we leave as friends?'

'Does it really matter?'

'Well, I don't want there to be any . . . sort of —'

'Oh, please, Bill, for God's sake, don't do the "hard feelings" line.'

'No, I just mean . . . Leigh, I wouldn't like to think —'

'I know exactly what you wouldn't like to think. Like every other bloody man. You wouldn't like to think that I have any negative feelings towards you. You'd like to think I still *like* you. You'd like to think I regard our time together as a magical little oasis in the desert of my life, on which I will look back fondly as I get older. Whatever happens, you don't want me to think badly of you.'

'Well . . .' She was embarrassingly close to the truth. 'What will you think of me, Leigh?'

'Bill, I think it's very unlikely that I will think about you at all.'

Chapter eighteen

... and, by way of contrast, a dentist in Tasmania has written his autobiography under the title 'A Bridge Too Far'.

The message on the answering machine was prickly and curt. Dewi had discussed Bill's request with Andrea and the children, and been persuaded — against his better judgment, the tone implied — that a visit would be permissible. It was scheduled for two-thirty to three pm the following Saturday. Dewi gave details of the hospital and ward where Andrea could be found.

Not the most welcoming of acquiescences. For a moment, Bill Stratton was tempted to let the opportunity pass. Andrea was now so far out of his life, why should he bother visiting her? He clearly wasn't wanted and, besides, he'd always had a squeamishness about hospitals. Whereas Andrea had seemed positively energised by their atmosphere, he had always tried to avoid visiting them. Even with a couple of closeish friends who'd died, Bill had taken the coward's way out towards the end, sending a card rather than appearing in person.

Had he been feeling his usual self, he probably would have given seeing Andrea a miss. But his encounter with Leigh the night before had left him raw, with an instinct for self-flagellation. He wouldn't enjoy going to the hospital to see Andrea. For that very reason, he must make the visit.

He left a message on Dewi's answering machine to that effect.

Bill Stratton's dentist had an hour a day set aside for emergencies. The broken tooth was reckoned to qualify and, after one look, the dentist announced that the offending molar should be removed.

'There's hardly any of it left, anyway. Mostly just old filling I'll be pulling out.' The dentist was Australian, reputed to be very charming to his female patients. He didn't bother with any of that for the men. 'Do you want an injection?'

'Yes, please.' Bill had never been that keen on pain.

The dentist sighed at his cowardice. 'Very well. But it'll come out with one tug. There's not much holding it in place.'

Bill was adamant. 'I'd still rather have the injection.'

'Fine.' The dentist made rather heavy weather of inserting the needle into the gum, and didn't disguise his impatience during the wait for the anaesthetic to take effect.

'That won't be the last one,' he said ominously.

'What?'

'The last tooth to come out. They're all in bad nick.'

'Oh, thank you.' Not only impotent, now my body's falling apart. 'What would you recommend?'

The dentist shrugged. 'Have them all out. Get dentures.'

The image wasn't appealing. Bill knew he should have looked after his teeth better over the years, but his squeamishness about medical establishments extended to dental surgeries as well as hospitals, so he had developed a bad habit of missing his regular check-ups.

The idea of dentures, though . . . of putting his smile in a glass overnight. Or didn't people do that anymore? There were enough advertisements for denture fixatives around . . . day-time television commercials featuring desperately enthusiastic, fit-looking pensioners of the kind who were about to realise the equity in their houses and would soon be equally keen on buying stairlifts and walk-in baths.

(As soon as he had the thought, Bill's mind returned to a question which always bugged him when he saw those commercials for walk-in baths. He wasn't stupid enough to think you fill the bath before you open the door but what he always wanted to know was: what happened when you emptied it? Presumably you just sat there, getting colder and colder, till the water got below the, sort of, doorstep level and you could walk out. Which might well explain why old people were so wrinkled.)

He brought himself back to thinking about denture fixative. Maybe they did now manufacture some that lasted twenty-four/seven? Maybe, like toupees, there were now false teeth that would not inhibit the wearer's normal life in any way . . . false teeth that could be worn in the shower . . . in heavy winds . . . even while making love? Bill still didn't like the idea of dentures, though; didn't like the image of himself as a resolutely smiling extra in a denture fixative commercial.

'I gather,' he said to the dentist, 'that there are alternatives to dentures these days.'

'Always have been.' He tapped one of Bill's teeth, none too gently, with a metal probe. 'Can you still feel that?'

'Yes,' he lied. He wanted to find out more

about the potential cosmetic solutions to his dental problem. 'But can't you get false teeth kind of . . . screwed into your gums?'

'That's not exactly the process, no.'

'Or veneers? A friend of mine has had veneers.'

'For veneers to work, the basic teeth have to be in good condition.' The dentist took a disparaging look into Bill's mouth. 'You might get away with veneers on the front ones. At the back, though, it looks like Dresden after the Allied bombing. That's going to need more structural work.'

'Do you do that?'

'No, but I know a very good cosmetic dentist if you'd like to be referred.' The answer was too practised; clearly there was some lucrative mutual back-scratching going on.

Bill said he would like to have the contact number.

'Right. Let's just get rid of this little stub first.' Bill's tooth received another healthy clout with the probe. 'Can't feel that, can you?'

Before there was time for a reply, a pair of what looked like pliers were inserted into Bill's mouth, there was a quick twist, and a lump of grey metal and yellowed tooth emerged.

'See — hardly any root there at all. You didn't need the injection.'

Which made Bill Stratton feel even more as though his body was quietly crumbling away.

The orthodontist was Australian too, confirming Bill's suspicion of some kind of connivance between them. Female, beautiful body in white work suit, whiteness continuing in pale make-up under sculpted black hair. But not fanciable; there was something too antiseptic about her. She had all the sex appeal of a cotton bud.

She inspected his mouth, calling out information to a junior cotton bud, who keyed it into a laptop. When she finished, her expression didn't change, but Bill got the strong feeling he hadn't passed the examination.

'Well, there are a lot of possibilities nowadays,' she announced. 'Presumably you want the bite straightened, apart from anything else?'

'What, and get rid of my "crooked smile"?'

'Sorry?'

'I've just always had this crooked smile. People expect it, when they see me. You know, when I do public appearances.'

'Ah.' She showed no interest in his celebrity. 'Well, I can reduplicate existing deficiencies, if required.'

'Well, I would like that existing deficiency reduplicated.'

'Fine.' She nodded to the junior cotton bud, who made a note on the laptop, and then passed across a bound album. 'I'd like to show you the kind of cosmetic work I can offer you.'

The 'before' photographs made him feel a bit better. Surely his dentition wasn't as bad as those. On the other hand, presumably she'd selected the worst cases, to show the wonderful transformations that her wizardry could achieve.

'A friend of mine,' Bill ventured, 'has just had veneers done, and she's very pleased with the result.'

'Yes, well, of course I do veneers.'

'So you're, kind of, a veneerologist?'

She wasn't amused. The junior cotton bud didn't crack a smile either. Bill got the impression they had both heard the line before. 'I'm an orthodontist,' she said sharply. 'Or cosmetic dentist, if you prefer.'

'Right.'

She then confirmed his dentist's view that veneers might work on Bill's front teeth, but more radical work would be needed at the back. She didn't use the Dresden analogy; she said the area looked like 'a scrap metal yard.'

'Would it be possible just to do the veneers, and leave the back as it is? I mean, nobody's going to see back there, are they?'

She winced at this affront to her professionalism. 'It would be possible, Mr Stratton, but it would be very unwise. Storing up even worse problems for you in the future.'

'Mmm, but I mean, out of interest . . . how much would just doing the veneers cost?'

She patently disapproved of answering the question, but did not refuse to do so. She went through a ritual with the junior cotton bud about finding the up-to-date price-list. 'We would of course be talking about porcelain veneers. There are others on the market made of cheaper materials, but I personally don't deal with them.'

'Right, porcelain it is. So how much would it cost?'

She told him. Bill let out a low whistle. 'Pricey.' He grinned. 'Still, if that sorts out my whole smile, I suppose it's not bad.'

'Mr Stratton, that is the price per tooth.'

His media career had inculcated the habit

of punctuality in Bill Stratton. The timing of news bulletins was not elastic, and he would always arrive in good time for his shifts. So he was at the hospital, with a rather tatty bunch of flowers bought from a nearby kiosk, soon after two on the Saturday afternoon.

He was interested to find that Andrea was being treated on a private ward. She and Dewi might be avid supporters of the NHS in conversation, but when it came to something really serious they paid for what they hoped would be the best.

He checked in with the nurse at the flower-bedecked ward reception and was told which room Mrs Roberts was in. Tea or coffee was offered — something else you get for paying extra — but he refused.

Bill breathed in deeply as he walked along the plushly-carpeted corridor, trying to quell his customary discomfort on hospital premises. The scent of the flowers could not quite mask the endemic smell of disinfectant. The décor was muted blues and purples; small chain hotel, one step above a Travelodge. Framed pictures on the walls were of swans on lakes and misty sunsets through trees.

He stopped outside a door in whose Perspex slot was a card reading 'Mrs Roberts'. Once again, he felt the urge to duck out, just to run and avoid the inevitable awkwardness. It wouldn't matter. Dewi and his family couldn't think less of him than they already did.

But he put away the cowardly thought, and tapped on the door.

A full minute elapsed before Dewi opened it. Though in the early days of their separation Andrea's lover had filled his thoughts, Bill had by now almost forgotten what the man looked like. He had not visualised the bushy eyebrows, the matching fringe of hair around the bald dome of his head, nor thought of Dewi's off-duty penchant for pastel pullovers in geometric designs, pale blue trousers and leather slip-ons with extraneous bits of metal on them.

'I said half past two.' The voice was heavy with Welsh pique. 'It's only twenty-two minutes past.'

'Yes, I'm sorry. I arrived early.'

'You could have waited. They do have chairs at reception.'

'Yes, but —'

'It doesn't matter, Dewi. Since he's here, let him come in.'

Bill Stratton could not believe the voice that emerged from the recesses of the room. Very light, working hard against some resistance, like a sea wind through thick dune grass. Only just recognisable as Andrea's.

Unwillingly, Dewi stood back to admit the unwelcome guest. Bill moved into the one-step-above-Travelodge private room.

If Andrea's voice had been a shock, the sight of her was a bigger one. Propped up on pillows, her thin arms made her look like nothing more than a stack of kindling. She was attached to a drip. Her brown eyes seemed disproportionately large in her yellow-grey face. He couldn't see the state of her hair, because she had tied a bright, defiant bandana around her head.

Bill didn't know what to do. His instinct was to go and give his ex-wife a kiss, but Dewi's glowering presence discouraged that. Also, Andrea looked so frail that a mere peck on the cheek might be too much for her.

So instead he held out his pathetic bunch of flowers.

'I'll take those.' Dewi did so. 'I've never been in favour of flowers in a sick room. The nurses'll look after them.'

But he didn't go off to reception. Instead, he sat down in a chair on one side of Andrea's bed. He maintained a defensive, proprietorial air. Bill hovered, uncertain whether he should take the chair on the other side of the bed, until Andrea wheezed, 'Do sit down.'

There was a silence. Bill desperately tried to think of something to say. All that came into his mind was a BWOC line from his after-dinner speaking routine. '. . . and, by way of contrast, before a big match an entire hospital football team developed chicken pox and had to scratch.' But he knew it wasn't the right moment for that.

'So, in for some tests . . . ?' he managed eventually.

This was so obvious that Andrea wasn't going to waste breath on answering it. She nodded.

'Any results yet?'

'Not final results, no,' Dewi replied. 'And if we did have them, they would be confidential, just for the family.'

All right, all right, thought Bill, you've made your point. I am no longer part of Andrea's life. I know that. He was surprised by Dewi's level of prickliness. Bill didn't flatter himself that he meant anything to Andrea now. Her second husband had no cause for anxiety. But Dewi still seemed very twitchy.

The silence seemed fated to continue for ever, so Bill asked, 'And they're treating you all right in here, are they?'

It was Dewi who replied. 'The staff are excellent. The performance figures for this hospital are the best in the area. That's why we chose it.'

'Fine, fine.' Again the silence looked as if it was going for a Personal Best.

Andrea broke it this time. 'Dewi,' she gasped, 'why don't you take the flowers to reception?'

'Well . . .' He was unwilling to abandon his sentry duty. He couldn't stand the idea of leaving his wife with her ex-husband.

'Please . . .'

With bad grace he conceded. He rose and walked away, holding Bill's flowers as though they were some dead rodent that needed binning. At the door he stopped and looked balefully at the visitor. 'You arrived here at twenty-two minutes past, so I'll be back at eight minutes to three.' The half-hour that had been negotiated. Bill would have bet that there was no slippage of appointment times in Dr. Roberts' surgery.

He looked at Andrea. There was a vagueness, a blurring in her prominent brown eyes. Presumably she was on heavy medication. 'I'm sorry. I can see my being here is upsetting Dewi. Perhaps I shouldn't have come.'

'Dewi'll get over it. Anyway, I wanted to

see you.' She didn't make it sound as though this were a heart-felt need, just a necessary chore.

'So, I mean, Andrea, you can tell me . . . what is the, er . . . I mean, what kind of . . . have they given you any indication . . . ?' The words tangled in his squeamishness about matters medical.

'What is the prognosis? Is that what you're trying to say?'

'Er, yes, I suppose it is.'

She shrugged. 'The consultant says fifty-fifty. Having nursed cases like this, I'd put it nearer sixty-forty against.' She spoke without emotion, ever the medical pragmatist. 'The thing is, if I am going to need surgery, then I'm going to have to build up my strength. But I think I'm in with a chance.' She paused to regather her breath. The long speech was taking it out of her. 'As you probably know, with cancer, mental attitude matters a lot. And I am very positive. I'm determined to get better . . . now that I've got so many things in my life to live for.'

Bill didn't need to ask for details. He didn't want to hear the manifold virtues of Dewi and his children catalogued. Nor did he want the contrast between her current status and her former life with him spelt out. From her tone it was clear that if she'd developed cancer while she was still married to him she would have given up the ghost with no struggle at all.

'And how are you?' she asked, more as a formal politeness than out of any great interest.

'Oh . . . well . . .' He tried to think of things in his life that he could tell her about. His recent impotence was hardly appropriate. And his dental troubles seemed singularly unimportant, given the scale on which Andrea was suffering. Nor did he think it was quite the moment to start listing his post-divorce sexual encounters. 'Not so bad,' he concluded feebly.

'Good.' She still didn't sound interested.

'I have been doing a lot more after-dinner speaking.'

'Oh, really?' There was a note of surprise in her voice.

'I mean, mostly based on old "by way of contrast" lines.'

'Ah. That would explain it.'

'Sorry?'

'Well, I can't imagine you coming up with any original material for after-dinner speeches.'

'Maybe not. Sal's set it all up. She's still acting as my agent.'

'Uh-huh.' She dismissed the news, as she

always had dismissed details of his professional life. Andrea still had the ability to make him feel very shallow and trivial. In fact, she could do it even more now she had the support of the infinitely worthy Dewi and his infinitely worthy children.

'And the only other person I really see from our former life is . . .' In spite of the unsatisfactory nature of their last meeting, he still felt a little bold saying the name '. . . Ginnie.'

'Oh God.' Andrea was surprised. 'Is she still as affected as ever?'

'Well, she's still a bit actressy, but I wouldn't have said she was affected.'

'Oh, she was. She always was. I never knew why you wanted to stay in touch with her.'

'*I* wanted to? She was your friend, Andrea.'

'No, she wasn't.'

'Oh, come on. From school onwards.'

'All right, I don't deny that I knew her before you did, and yes, she was my friend actually *at* school, but afterwards . . . no, it was you who kept wanting to include her in everything we were doing.'

'That's not how I remember it.'

'Your memory always was conveniently selective, Bill.'

'But —'

'You're not having an *affair* with Ginnie, are you?'

'Good God, no.'

'Well, perhaps you should.' For a moment Andrea sounded almost sympathetic.

'I don't think —'

The moment of sympathy passed, as she went on, 'You're both as shallow as each other.'

'Oh.'

Her breathing was getting difficult again. 'Anyway, I'm glad you're all right, Bill. We're both so much better off apart.'

'Maybe.'

'We should never have got married. Amazing, thinking back, how much pressure there was to do that, even in the sixties. Doing what one *should,* doing the proper thing. What a lot of time we wasted.'

'I don't think it was all wasted, Andrea.'

'Well, I do. Still, at least — thank God, better late than never — I've found out what a happy marriage can be like.'

With that stuck-up prig, Dewi? Not the moment to express the opinion, though.

'That's why I'm going to get better,' Andrea wheezed. 'I've got every reason to live.'

'Yes, yes, of course you have,' he agreed automatically.

Bill tried to think of other things to say. Nothing offered itself. Normally, when conversation lay becalmed, he would ease the atmosphere with a few 'by way of contrast' lines. But Andrea had never been amused by them while they were together, and he didn't think the influence of Dewi would have changed her attitude.

'Presumably, this cancer . . .' he said at last, 'was caused by passive smoking?'

'What?'

'All your nursing friends. You know, if you think of the amount they used to smoke round that big kitchen table in Putney, they —'

'My cancer,' Andrea breathed imperiously, 'has been sent to test me. I don't know where it came from, but it's a challenge. And it's a challenge I'm going to win.'

'Ah. Good.'

'Anyway, I'm glad you're all right, Bill —'

'Well, all right*ish*.'

'It'd be nice to think that we've both managed to move on after that disastrous marriage.'

'Now, just a minute. I think you are exaggerating a bit there. Okay, our marriage wasn't perfect —'

'You can say that again.'

'— but I think "disastrous" is a bit strong.'

'That's the word I'd use.'

'Why, Andrea? What was wrong with it?'

'*You* were wrong with it, Bill. It was all right while we were engaged, but the minute we got married...' She gasped for breath.

'What happened the minute we got married?'

'You instantly became jealous, possessive and controlling. You were always watching what I was doing, and you were deeply resentful of any attempts I made to set up anything that didn't involve you.' She panted, running out of air, but still determined to finish her catalogue of grievances. 'You used to constantly criticise my appearance and my home-making skills. And your sole aim in life was to totally undermine my confidence.'

Bill Stratton didn't recognise any part of himself in that description. But then, presumably, nor did any of the world's other ex-husbands.

He left the hospital before the end of the half-hour Dewi had allotted for him.

Chapter nineteen

. . . and, by way of contrast, an advertisement for a second-hand hearse in a South African newspaper said it had fifteen thousand miles on the clock and a carefully maintained body.

Andrea died ten days later. She never went home from the hospital. Nothing wrong with her will to resist the challenge. That was strong, but the cancer was stronger.

Bill Stratton received the information in a phone-call from one of Dewi's sons. His father, he explained, was too upset to talk to everyone. Dewi had done the immediate family, but the children were working through the 'other names in Andrea's address book'. They certainly knew how to rub it in, thought Bill. The son's accent, though not Welsh, carried the same overtone of offended righteousness as the father's.

Bill came up with some appropriate form of condolence to be passed on to Dewi, and asked about funeral arrangements. The son said they weren't finally settled yet. Bill said he'd be grateful to be informed when they were. The son reluctantly agreed to pass on

264

the information. He made it clear, however, that 'the family' would find the event quite difficult enough without having Andrea's ex-husband around as an additional irritant. But they would let him know.

The phone call left Bill numb. He was not unfeeling about his ex-wife's death, but he knew that the details of what he felt would take a long time to shake down. For the time being, numbness would have to do. He was also aware of the incongruity of his situation. If Andrea's cancer had been diagnosed two years earlier, the crisis would have been on his watch. Bill Stratton's wife would have been faced with a potentially terminal disease, and Bill Stratton himself would have done all the things a dutiful husband should. (In spite of what Andrea had said about him, Bill did still think of himself as having been a dutiful husband.) It would have been he who reacted with horror to the diagnosis, who waited agonisingly for the results of tests, supported her through the debilitating effects of chemotherapy, and sat by her side through the long, losing struggle for her life. And their friends would have been as supportive as they could, would have empathised with their sufferings, would have felt respect and compassion for Bill Stratton's stoicism in the hour of ultimate challenge.

Whereas now . . . all that sympathy would be lavished on Dewi Roberts. He would be the sufferer and the saint. Which was, Bill had to concede, entirely fair. Dewi was the one who'd been there to support his wife through the ghastly leaving of this world. And it was a job that, with his medical skills and trained bedside manner, he probably did a lot better than Bill would have done.

The ramifications of all this, however, could not fail to affect the way Andrea's ex-husband was seen. Bill Stratton would become something close to the villain of the piece. Not only had he been such an unsatisfactory husband that Andrea had had to divorce him, but he had also shown no interest in her declining health. He had only gone to see her once in hospital, very near the end. The fact that no one had told him she was ill would be lost in the general censoriousness. Any available blame would be showered on the shiftless ex-husband rather than the sainted Dewi.

For a man like Bill Stratton, whose main motive in life was to be liked, the prospect was unappealing.

Also, below all the feelings of shock and guilt and pain, he could not suppress a slight feeling of injustice. He was the one

266

who'd put in the groundwork. He'd spent nearly forty years married to Andrea . . . and the relationship hadn't been nearly as bad as she maintained. Bill had worked at the marriage. And then suddenly, in what turned out to be the last couple of years of her life, Dewi had swanned in to receive all the plaudits . . . like the Americans coming in late in a war to get all the glory.

Bill Stratton knew such thoughts were unworthy . . . particularly in the circumstances . . . but he could not suppress them. As well as feeling numb, he felt aggrieved.

There were people he should ring. Sal, Carolyn and Trevor had never been that close to Andrea — there was no hurry to tell them — but Ginnie . . . in spite of what Andrea had said, the two women had been very close at one point in their lives. He should dial that mobile number in Croatia.

But not yet. Bill decided to take his numbness down to the pub, see if alcohol might release some of the confused emotions inside him.

The mobile in Croatia was on voicemail. He didn't leave any details, just asked her to call him. Then he lay down to sleep off too many pints at lunchtime.

The telephone woke him, but it wasn't

Ginnie. It was Sal. She'd heard about Andrea.

'How on earth do you know everything so quickly?'

'I keep my ear to the ground.'

Bill should have expected that. Sal's 'ear to the ground' had also found out about many of his sexual encounters.

She pronounced some formal sentiments of condolence and then said, 'But how do you feel about it, Bill?'

'I honestly don't know.'

Which was true.

The phone rang again almost immediately after he'd finished talking to Sal. Still not Ginnie. Dewi's daughter this time — they were sharing out the disagreeable tasks — giving him funeral details, as requested. Three pm the following Tuesday. At a chapel in Muswell Hill. But Bill didn't need to feel he had to attend.

Her tone, again not Welsh but again imbued with Dewi's righteousness, which only just stopped short of telling him not to come, made Bill all the more determined that he should be there. Even that afternoon, unbidden images of Andrea had come into his mind, many from long ago, from the time when they'd first met. All right, the marriage hadn't worked out, but they'd been together nearly four decades. He was damned if he was going to forget her just like that, on the orders of some jumped-up little Welsh GP.

It was early evening when Ginnie finally got through. A couple of hours later in Croatia. They'd just finished the day's shooting. 'I am in rather a rush, Bill. Going out for dinner.'

'Don't worry. It won't take long. Andrea's dead.'

'Oh, *darling* . . .' The word extended almost infinitely.

'Lung cancer. It was very quick towards the end.'

'Oh, *my God* . . .'

'Look, I just wanted you to know.'

'Oh, thank you so much, Bill. I'm just *devastated*. But you . . . you poor darling . . . how are you feeling?'

The original answer was still true. 'I honestly don't know.'

Then he moved on quickly to what he really wanted to tell her. If Dewi's family wanted to squeeze him out of the funeral, let them. He'd have his revenge. If he turned up to the chapel with one of the country's most famous actresses, having maybe had a nice *tête-à-tête* lunch beforehand . . . well, that would show them. He wasn't just

Andrea's reject. Bill Stratton was something of a celebrity, moving in the circles of even bigger celebrities.

He told Ginnie the time of the funeral.

'Oh, darling, I'd love to be able to make it —'

'Surely, for something like that, the schedule could be re-arranged. I mean, you knew Andrea longer than I did.'

'Yes, yes, it's not that, Bill. In fact, we do have a break next week, I'm free Sunday to Thursday —'

'Well, there you are — it fits in fine.'

'Trouble is . . . I have *made plans* . . .' Her voice dropped to its sultriest. 'Plans that I really can't change. The fact is, I don't know if you know Dickie Burns . . . ?'

'I don't think I do.'

'Well, he's been out here being a guest on a couple of episodes . . . playing a knight just back from the Crusades . . . done a lovely job, and been an absolute hoot on the set. Anyway, I don't know if you knew that Dickie and I had a thing yonks ago?'

'No, I didn't.'

'Well, it's, sort of . . . not exactly started up again, but . . .' She giggled with deliberate throaty ambiguity. 'No, no, we're just having a fun time, no commitments, you know . . . and Dickie's had this wonderful romantic idea that we take advantage of the break in the shooting to have a few days on Krk.'

'Where?'

'Krk. It's the biggest Croatian island. Anyway, Dickie knows this wonderful little quaint olde-worlde hotel there, and God, we could both do with a break and —'

'A romantic break?'

'Just a break, darling.' He didn't know whether he could believe her. The excitement in her voice was at odds with her words.

'So you won't be coming to the funeral?'

'Darling, how can I . . . in the circumstances?'

'You did know Andrea for over forty years.'

'I know, Bill. But I never liked her that much. You were always the reason why I stayed in touch. You were the one who mattered to me.'

Somehow Bill didn't find that news as comforting as he might have done before Dickie Burns' name had been mentioned.

Sal was there at the chapel in Muswell Hill. And Carolyn. Even Trevor had turned up. Bill and Andrea had sometimes gone out as foursomes with him and the current wife. He seemed to feel the need to pay his respects, anyway.

The one person who wasn't there was Andrea. Not in the sense that she was dead. In the sense that no vestige of her body was actually in the chapel. There had been a cremation service in the morning, 'just for the immediate family'. All that remained of Bill Stratton's ex-wife was now just smoke and indissoluble solids.

He hadn't had his nice *tête-à-tête* lunch. Sal had rung, suggesting grabbing a quick bite before the funeral, 'if he felt like it'. Trevor had offered to meet up for a couple of pints, 'if he felt like it'. Even Carolyn — to Bill's considerable surprise — had rung and said that rather than walking into the chapel alone, she'd be happy to join up with him, 'if he felt like it'.

But Bill Stratton didn't feel like it. In the days before the funeral, images of Andrea in his mind became frequent and more confusing. He didn't know what he wanted, except to be on his own. He wasn't looking forward to the ceremony, but he would be there and somehow get through it. It was something he knew he should do. But he didn't want the sympathy or banter of his friends. What he needed to do was to find out what Andrea's death had made him feel.

And that was a task he had to deal with on his own.

The funeral service began. And just as Andrea's physical presence had been edited out of the chapel, so had her life before she came together with Dewi Roberts been edited out of her history.

Bill was slightly drunk; not out of control, but headachey. Ever the good time-keeper, he'd arrived at a nearby pub at one-thirty. He hadn't wanted to put his bladder at risk during the service by taking in a lot of fluid, so he'd drunk Scotch. He'd also ordered fish and chips, but when it arrived, a slab of grey matter encased in something that looked and tasted like the cardboard centre of a toilet roll, he'd ceased to feel hungry. So all he had inside him was three double Scotches.

Having lurked as long as possible in the small park opposite the chapel, Bill had been one of the last to enter. He'd seen Sal arrive, and Carolyn and Trevor, but again rejected the easy option of joining any one of them. As a result, he was installed at the end of a pew in the back row, ready for a quick getaway if his nerve failed.

But his late entrance and obscure seat did not prevent Bill Stratton from being observed by the congregation. A few necks craned round before the service actually began. One or two of the faces he recognised from their days of whingeing about the NHS around the Putney kitchen table. He couldn't hear the whispered comments that were being passed round, but he reckoned they were along the lines of 'That's the first husband, *the man who done her wrong.*'

Bill had only ever seen his ex-wife inside a church at their own wedding and the subsequent weddings of friends, but the unctuous minister conducting the service spoke of her as 'a member of our congregation here in Muswell Hill and very dear friend to many of us present today'. Maybe he said that at every funeral, whether he'd known the victim or not, but he did seem to be familiar with Andrea and her life. Had marriage to Dewi brought her to God as well as vegetarianism?

It was so long since Bill himself had been inside a church that he couldn't tell whether the service was a standard one or the ritual of some obscure denomination. He should have looked at the board outside. He thought he detected an air of Welshness, if only in the gusto with which the obscure hymns were being belted out. The language of the liturgy was clunkingly modern. At times he almost recognised long-forgotten quotes from The Book of Common Prayer, awkwardly rendered into lines devoid of rhythm and cadence.

But it was the tributes, the eulogies, that really stuck in his gullet. First, Dewi's youngest child, a daughter — though not the one who had rung Bill — read an extract 'from one of Andrea's all-time favourite books, *The Alchemist: A Fable about Following Your Dream* by Paulo Coelho'. Bill had never heard of it. He'd lived with Andrea for nearly forty years and she'd never mentioned the book. There certainly had never been a copy in any of their houses. So to call it one of her *recent* favourite books might have been just about acceptable; 'all-time favourite' was, Bill reckoned, pushing at the boundaries of truth.

Nor did he warm to the content of what was read. New Age mush, to his mind. He'd never had any taste for allegory. Still, the reading had one positive effect. Now he'd heard a sample, there was no danger he was ever going to read the rest of *The Alchemist*.

The second interlude between the slabs of service was even worse. Dewi's older daughter and his son, the two who'd spoken to Bill on the phone, sang and played guitar — they would do — and they'd written a song 'specially for this occasion, not to dwell on the sadness of Andrea's death, but to celebrate the joy of her life!' The entire congregation — with one significant exception — seemed deeply touched by this gesture, and waited with rapt attention for the music to begin.

Bill found the song frankly insulting. Particularly the verse that went:

> She was our new mother, more or
> less,
> And our father's loving wife,
> Though, sadly, she only found
> happiness
> In the last three years of her life.

Not only were the lyrics offensive, but the music was dreadful, in the way that only modern Christian music can be, sort of by Cliff Richard out of Peter, Paul and Mary.

If he'd thought the song was bad, worse was to follow, in the form of 'memories of Andrea' from Glyn, 'a family friend'. Glyn started by saying that Dewi had wanted to do this part of the service, but he 'didn't trust himself to get through it without blubbing'. The congregation let out a communal sigh of concern for the grieving widower. What about me, Bill demanded silently, I'm a grieving widower too. Yes, I know this is the second time Dewi's been through it, and I'm very sorry for the repellent prig, but I should get a look-in. I loved Andrea too.

This was the first time since their split-up that he had shaped that thought, and it shocked him. But there was a sobering truth in it.

Numbly, in pain, he listened to the address. The woman Glyn described bore no relation to the Andrea he had known. Her compassion, her caring nature, the way she had embraced Welsh culture, her selfless love for Dewi and his children . . . Bill recognised none of it.

As in the song, though, Glyn too had a sideways knock at the ex-husband. 'And what makes her death all the sadder,' he concluded, 'is that Andrea had so recently found her real self, had so recently found the happiness and fulfilment she so richly deserved. Essentially loyal, but locked for many years into a marriage that cramped her magnificent style, it was only once she and Dewi became a team that Andrea could finally express the beauty of her personality. We will all miss her dreadfully.'

Bill Stratton now knew what it felt like to be one of Stalin's former henchmen, airbrushed out of history.

Another unfamiliar hymn was belted out with Welsh brio, more awkwardly-phrased prayers were said. Then the minister encouraged everyone to go back 'to the Roberts family home for a drink and a chance to talk about the wonderful woman we have so sadly lost today, but who has gone on to a greater happiness than our mere mortal imaginations can envisage'. Suddenly the organ was playing get-out music.

Sod any convention that the grieving family leaves the church first. Bill Stratton's only desire was to be out of the place before he had to see anyone. He took immediate advantage of his well-chosen seat and made for the door.

He was through the churchyard and out of the gate before he heard the clatter of high heels behind him, and a voice calling his name.

He recognised Carolyn, and turned to face her.

'Wondered if you fancied a drink . . . ?' she said, as she lit up a much-needed cigarette.

'If you think I'm going back to join the cosiness of "the family home", then you —'

'I wasn't thinking that. Meant a pub.'

'Well, I . . . thank you, but I don't think I can.'

She was piqued. 'Please yourself.'

'I mean, it's not that I . . . I just . . .' He looked up with horror to see Dewi, his children and the minister emerging from the chapel doors. And he said something that seemed to encapsulate his whole life at that moment. 'I don't know what to do.'

'Take up smoking.' Carolyn, her annoyance gone, took the cigarette she had just lit out of her mouth and pressed it into his.

'But I don't smoke.'

'You do now.'

Conscious of the slight greasiness of her lipstick on the filter tip, Bill drew in the warm acrid taste. It was obscurely comforting.

There was more compassion than he'd ever seen in Carolyn's blue eyes as she lit up another cigarette for herself and said, 'So do you want to go and have a drink or something?'

He did. 'I do.' But at the same time he didn't. The congregation was spilling out of the church around the grieving Robertses. He had to go. 'But no. Thank you, but I need to be alone at the moment.'

'Okay.'

Carolyn watched him as, puffing determinedly on his cigarette, he walked off down the road towards the tube station.

Chapter twenty

. . . and, by way of contrast, a pot-holer who was rescued from a cave after eight days said he survived — rather appropriately — on a diet of pot noodles.

His late ex-wife had condemned Bill Stratton as shallow, but even shallow people have depths. And during the weeks after Andrea's funeral he plumbed those depths. He was probably not spiritually equipped to have a Dark Night of the Soul in the full St John of the Cross version, but his soul did go through a distinctly greyish period.

Bill thought about his whole life, and how he'd spent it, and he wasn't over-impressed with himself. As well as shallow, he felt hollow. He even disparaged the personal anguish that he felt. He was suffering, but a more sensitive person would be suffering more. Dewi Roberts, he felt certain, was achieving a much more noble and admirable depth of suffering.

The trouble, Bill Stratton now realised, was that he had always kept his emotions at a distance. As a newsreader, he had been a conduit for disasters which had left him personally untouched and unmoved. He had looked suitably grave as he announced bomb outrages, famines, earthquakes and the deaths of international icons. But the very act of speaking them out loud had somehow inured him to their impact.

It wasn't only in his professional career that he had been a conduit. As an after-dinner speaker, he was a conduit for old 'by way of contrast' lines. And at times he suspected that he was no more than a conduit for his personal emotions too. They went straight through him; they didn't touch the sides.

Andrea's death had shaken him to his foundations, but in his slough of self-hatred, he didn't feel his grieving was adequate. All he felt was a constant, dull unhappiness. He went through the motions of life, he delivered 'by way of contrast' lines in after-dinner speeches on automatic pilot. But whatever opportunities presented themselves, he felt no urge to make contact with any women.

That was the part of his life that Andrea's death had made him feel worst about. While he'd felt no guilt at all during his flurry of pick-ups and sexual encounters, every one of them now felt like a cavalier betrayal of

Andrea, or of something. In retrospect he was appalled by his callow chat-up routines borrowed from the BWOC archive, by the love-making itself, by the smug hypocrisy of his conscience-salving Interflora gifts with their cocky little cards of thanks. What had become of the real Bill Stratton during that time? What had he been doing, for God's sake? *Was* there a real Bill Stratton?

He determined that that was the end, so far as women were concerned. He wasn't to be trusted with them. All he was capable of was bringing them unhappiness. He had never felt lower.

Sal no doubt would have told him, after a reading of *Referred Pain: How We Take It Out on Those We Love* or something similar, that the reason he felt so bad was because he had never allowed himself time to grieve for his divorce. That now he was not just mourning Andrea's death, he was mourning the death of their marriage too. Sal might also, after reading something like *Blanket Coverage: How We Cosy Up for Comfort in Relationships*, have pointed out to him that Andrea had been his sheet anchor. Because he hadn't grown away from her emotionally, he had not had a problem with passionless promiscuity. For the same reason, he had preferred anonymous one-night stands to encounters in which his feelings were in danger of being engaged.

But Sal didn't have the opportunity to tell Bill any of that, because he didn't see her. During those weeks he didn't see anyone he didn't have to.

Sadly, one of the people he did have to see was the senior Australian cotton bud at the cosmetic dental clinic. She had conceded that, if he had some major structural work on the bombsite at the back of his mouth, she would be willing to put porcelain veneers on his teeth at the front. The work would take a lot of visits and the cost would be astronomical.

Bill didn't exactly decide to go along with her proposal, he was in too diminished a state to make decisions, but the effort of saying no seemed even more stressful than agreeing. So he found himself caught up in a long process of measuring and drilling and chipping and grinding and being told what a pity it was he hadn't looked after his teeth. All with the purpose of undoing the ravages of time. Except that the work wasn't really undoing them; it was hiding them.

Veneers. He was all too aware of their symbolism in relation to his life.

★ ★ ★

Bill Stratton felt really old now, felt every one of his sixty-odd years. He was on the final lap. There was not a lot more to look forward to. Even though he had embarked on a hideously expensive course of cosmetic dentistry, in other ways he let himself go. The visits to the gym stopped completely, shaving was reduced to two or three times a week, and he started drinking more than he had before. It didn't matter. Nothing mattered.

Hangovers made him ache all over in the mornings, reinforcing the sensation that his body was literally crumbling around him. The booze made him pee a lot too, prompting thoughts that he might have prostate cancer. This produced no panic; part of him almost welcomed the idea. And he drank more to speed the process of self-destruction.

More than once he was almost too drunk to do an after-dinner speaking gig. Only the relentless familiarity of the material kept him going. He knew that his words were slurring. Something new for the organisers to snigger at in their post-mortems with Sal.

When she rang him and left messages — he had the phone permanently in answering machine mode these days — he didn't return her calls. She could e-mail him the basic information about bookings and venues. He didn't go to the BWOC office either, and didn't call back on the two occasions when Carolyn made contact. He didn't even respond to Ginnie when she called. And he certainly didn't ring Trevor back. Drinking in The Annexe with a fellow depressive was far too cushy a solution. Bill Stratton wanted to indulge his misery on his own.

He became obsessed by how old he was, and the British press's fanaticism about putting everyone's age after their name fed his obsession. Everything worth achieving, he could see from his newspaper, was being achieved by people younger than him. And the rare over-sixties who did anything worthwhile only brought home to Bill his own comparative inadequacy. He found himself trying to assess the age of everyone he saw, and he had another very ugly moment on the tube.

He was travelling back to Pimlico after a lunchtime speaking engagement. He'd had too much to drink, but just about got away with it. He'd even felt quite bouncy and on top of things at the lunch. But the minute he was on his own on the tube, depression descended like a safety curtain in a theatre. Fancy being the oldest man on the tube, he mused. And then thought, no, I don't fancy being the oldest man on the tube. He looked around the compartment. There was a baldish man slightly to his left. But baldness happens to people in their early twenties. The man was trying to dress younger than his age, but what was that age? Difficult to judge, but regretfully Bill had to concede it was probably under fifty. With increasing paranoia, he took another scan around the compartment. It didn't look good. He was stuck in a metal cylinder with a lot of people, all of whom were younger than he was. Come on, please, his mind screamed, please, someone older than me get on at the next stop. I don't care who it is . . . any old dosser will do . . . so long as he's older than me . . . so long as I'm not left as the oldest man on the tube!

His face, imperfectly reflected in the window opposite, now looked like a skull.

One of the advantages of being shallow is that plumbing your depths doesn't take as long as it would with someone less shallow. And, after some six weeks of misery and doubt, Bill Stratton did start to feel better.

The restoration of his self-esteem did not

happen overnight. The process was slow, but once started, his improvement accelerated. The first thing he did was to cut down his drinking. That was not as hard as it would have been for a more addictive personality. At the centre of Bill Stratton there had always been a core of self that hated losing control, and he recognised that his recent alcoholic excesses had arisen more from maudlin wallowing in self-abasement than from chemical compulsion. Then he resumed his visits to the gym. At first the work-outs were very hard, but gradually the regimen felt easier. He was basically in pretty good condition for a man in his early sixties.

Slowly he emerged from the pall that Andrea's death had cast over him. Soon, he thought, he would get in touch with people again. Women, even. He would no longer be looking for sex, or even love, but he could get back to having friendships with women. Yes, that was the answer. Soon he'd get back to being himself. Bill Stratton. Even enjoying being himself. He had no illusions about the qualities of his personality. But he knew he wasn't quite as bad as he'd thought himself over the previous six weeks.

One tragic death, you see, is not enough

to break a lifetime's habits of triviality. After Andrea died, Bill Stratton was not transformed. He did not see the light and immediately leave for Africa to do good works. But, to give him his due, he did set up a ten pounds a month standing order to Cancer Research.

Chapter twenty-one

. . . and, by way of contrast, a Gosport man who crawled home after a heavy session in the pub only realised the following morning that he'd left his wheelchair there.

'Kingsley Amis,' said Trevor, 'Kingsley Amis reckoned women were mad. It's in one of his later books, can't remember which one . . . well, it's in most of his later books probably . . . and a lot of the early ones. He reckoned they actually have a medical condition that makes them incapable of reasonable thought.'

'He always was a bit of a misogynist.'

'Oh yes, I agree, Bill, he was, but, you know, the more dealings I have with women, the more I reckon he may have had a point.'

'But I thought you didn't have any dealings with women nowadays.'

'Not voluntarily, no. But it's amazing how they still manage to infiltrate my life.'

'The ex-wives?'

'Them. And the daughters too. They just will not allow me any peace. God, I thought life'd be simpler when I got to my age.'

'You didn't exactly go out of your way to make it simpler, did you?'

'How do you mean?' Trevor sounded aggrieved.

'All the marriages, all the girlfriends.'

'Ah, yes, but I know why that was now.'

'Oh?'

'I've got an addictive personality.'

'Right.' Had Trevor taken a leaf out of Sal's book, and started reading self-help manuals?

'Yes. You see, if I start something, I go on with it, even if all the evidence shows it's not doing me any good.'

Bill pointed to Trevor's pint. 'That's certainly true.'

'I wasn't talking about the booze. I'm talking about women.'

'You're going to have to explain that.'

'Look, the situation is . . . I'm actually allergic to women.'

'Allergic?'

'Yes, they don't do me any good. I actually have a physical reaction when I'm with them.'

'So do all of us, if we get lucky.'

'Bill, will you please not trivialise this.' That was rich, coming from Trevor. 'An addictive personality is drawn to things that do them harm. I should never have messed with women at all.'

'Your ex-wives would agree with you there.'

'But I had no control. My addictive personality kept dragging me towards them. Even though a part of me knew I wasn't doing myself any good. The impulse was stronger than I was, you see.' He spread his hands wide in a gesture of innocence. 'So I can't be blamed for anything that happened. It wasn't my fault.'

As a justification for Trevor's behaviour — or that of any other man — that took some beating. But Bill, being a man, couldn't help being a little bit attracted to the theory.

'Where did you come across this idea?'

'It was in the *Daily Mail*,' Trevor replied piously, 'so it must be true.'

'Hmm. So you reckon, if you'd never got involved with any women at all, your life would have been better?'

'Obviously. I would have been much more successful in my career. I would have made a lot more money — and kept a lot more of what I did make. No, it's women who ruined everything for me.' At this bleak conclusion, Trevor took a deeply satisfied swig.

'So from now on you're just going to concentrate on that — your new addiction?'

'It's not new. I always drank.'

'Yes, but in the old days you used occasionally to do something other than drink.'

'Hmm. And now I don't have to.' Trevor smiled complacently. 'Not all bad, is it?'

'So didn't the *Daily Mail* reckon that your drinking was also a reflection of your obsessive personality?'

'Oh yes, probably. But it does me much more good.' He looked fondly at his glass. 'I mean, I've always got much more logic out of a pint than I ever have out of a woman.'

'Hmm.'

'Anyway, let's raise our glasses, Bill . . .'

'To what?'

'To you having seen the light as well.'

'Which light are you referring to?'

'The light that spells out in big neon letters: "WOMEN DON'T DO YOU NO GOOD." '

'Ah.'

'Well, come on. That's what you said.'

'I said that I wasn't intending to have any more emotional relationships with women.'

'Exactly. As I say, you've seen the light. Now you can be properly enrolled as the second full-time member of "The Annexe Misogynists' Club".'

'What would that involve?' Bill asked cautiously.

'Just doing more of what we do now. Meeting up here for as many drinks as we feel like, and stopping every now and then to raise our glasses to the lucky escape we've had from the perfidy of womankind.'

Bill saw exactly what Trevor had in mind, and the idea was not without appeal. Two old codgers tucked in the corner of a bar, complicit in their masculinity, safely sealed away from the emotional storms of inter-gender relationships. Such a life could get boring at times, but alcohol can be quite as effective as procrastination in the role of 'thief of time'. The Annexe would make a very effective fortress against the real world.

And for Trevor, how attractive that scenario would be. No more lonely drinking. An ever-present friend to share his moans, to stir the depths of his depressions. And to join in his castigations of the gender that had caused so much devastation in his life.

Yes, Bill could see the attraction.

But it did have one big drawback.

At some level, very deep down, even now, Bill did like women.

When he staggered back to Pimlico, at the end of a very long session with Trevor, there was a message from Virginia Fairbrother. The series had come to an end. She was hanging up her wimple, and would shortly be back in London.

Chapter twenty-two

. . . and, by way of contrast, scientists testing the theory that the best place to hide is nearest the light have concluded that it doesn't work for moths.

The restaurant this time wasn't trendy, just an Italian in Pimlico that Bill used fairly regularly. There was no likelihood of seeing anyone famous there. He hadn't even thought it posh enough as a venue to take Leigh to. But Ginnie had said she wanted something really simple. After months of eating *en masse* with all the Sister Saga cast and crew, she craved quiet.

Even her costume was more subdued. A well-cut but anonymous black trouser suit, a silver-grey scarf. She didn't want to make an entrance, she didn't want to be 'Virginia Fairbrother the famous actress'. She just wanted to have a quiet meal with an old friend.

Bill knew he wasn't looking his best. Though he had started back on his gym routine, he hadn't yet lost all the weight he'd accumulated during the post-funeral slump. His teeth also looked odd. The grinding process had been done, but the proper porcelain veneers had yet to be attached. As a result his teeth were wearing temporary plastic covers, of which he felt very self-conscious.

He mentioned the way he looked before Ginnie had a chance to. Get that over with.

'Oh, don't worry,' she said huskily. 'I look dreadful too.' From where Bill was sitting this was patently untrue. She looked absolutely gorgeous. 'Quite honestly, I'm still wiped out by all that filming. They're cutting so many corners in television these days that the schedule's ridiculous. We were often doing twelve- and fourteen-hour days, and still, of course, no proper rehearsal time.'

'But you had the odd break.'

'Very few.'

'You went to Krk.'

'Oh yes. Managed to fit that in.'

'With Dickie Burns.' Though he had given up all thoughts of relationships with women, Bill could still feel jealousy. 'So how was it?'

'Not marvellous. Rained most of the time.'

'Still, it must have been nice for you to be with Dickie.'

Ginnie's mobile face produced a grimace

which gave Bill enormous encouragement. 'He's a bit of a bore, to be quite honest. And he's not dealing with age as well as you and I are.'

'Oh?'

'Bit of the old mutton-dressed-as-lamb syndrome, poor Dickie. Because he always was the matinee idol type, he thinks he's still got this fatal attraction for women. But I'm afraid whatever he used to have in the way of looks has gone . . . as have other of his woman-attracting qualities . . .'

'What do you mean?'

'Even Viagra doesn't do it for him.'

While this was, in one way, encouraging news, it also necessitated the uncomfortable question: how did Ginnie know? So Bill asked it.

'Oh, purely anecdotal.' She was such a good actress it was impossible for him to know whether or not she was lying. 'But I think it's true. One of the make-up girls told me. He'd come on to her.'

'And presumably he came on to you too?'

'God, no.'

'I thought you were having a romantic break on Krk.'

'Just a break in filming. No romance involved.'

'But I thought you and Dickie had had a fling at one time.'

'At one time, yes.'

'And you didn't just pick up where you'd left off when you were on Krk?'

'God, no, darling. How many times do I have to tell you?' Again Bill wanted to believe her, but couldn't been sure. He remembered how giggly she'd sounded when telling him why she couldn't attend Andrea's funeral.

'I've got very few rules in my love life,' she went on. 'One is no sex without the possibility of love. The other is: never go back. A relationship that ended in tears once is — however hard you work to resuscitate it — always going to end in tears.'

'So you and Dickie didn't — ?'

'I spent my time with Dickie on Krk inside dreary little bars, listening to the rain pelting down and him going on and on about how old he felt.'

'Ah.'

'You almost sounded relieved there, Bill.'

'Well . . . when I rang you to tell you about Andrea's death, you were just about to go off to Krk and . . . well, for one thing I was disappointed that you wouldn't be able to come to the funeral, and, well . . .' He hesitated for a moment, then went for it '. . . you made it sound as if you and Dickie were going off to, well . . . to rekindle your love affair.'

'Me and Dickie?' She let out a throaty laugh at the incongruity of the pairing. Then she stopped and, turning the full beam of her hazel eyes on Bill, said, 'Mind you, I'm touched that you cared.'

'Well . . .' Why not say it? 'I did.'

Their eyes locked, and the contact was only broken when the waiter came to take their order. He knew Bill as a regular, and there was much coy laughing and Signor Strattoning. Ginnie said she hadn't the strength to make even the feeblest decision, and asked Bill to order for her. He suggested what he was going to have, his usual Parma Ham and Melon followed by Spaghetti Carbonara. Ginnie said that sounded divine.

When the waiter had gone, she reached her long thin hand across the table and placed it on top of Bill's. 'I'm sorry about the funeral. What I said about the trip to Krk was true, but nothing had been booked at that stage. Dickie had suggested our going there, and I saw it as a potential escape route. I just . . . I don't know, I didn't think I could face everyone at the funeral. I thought I'd give it a miss.'

'Very wise decision. I wish I'd done the same.'

'So . . . don't tell me if you don't want to, but how was it?'

Bill found he did want to tell her. He hadn't discussed the funeral with anyone and, without realising, had bottled up a lot of resentment on the subject. So he gave Ginnie a blow-by-blow account, from the moment he had entered the chapel, to the disapprobation of most of the congregation.

As he developed his narrative, he found the experience not only cathartic, but also profoundly funny. The absence of any trace of Andrea, the po-facedness of the mourners, the priggishness of the Roberts family — everything suddenly seemed hilarious. Bill knew he was exaggerating the awfulness, but, rewarded by the tears of laughter trickling down Ginnie's cheeks, could not help himself from embroidering the story even more. When he quoted the lyrics of the song specially composed by Dewi's children, she became incapacitated with laughter.

'Signor Stratton, I thought you do your funny talking after dinner, not before,' said the approaching waiter.

'Sometimes both,' Bill managed to say through his giggles.

He realised that only the arrival of the

starters had caused Ginnie to remove her hand from his. Otherwise, it had been there right through his funeral routine. He smiled across at her. He felt hugely relieved at having got all that off his chest, at having vented his spleen. Yes, he was being unfair to Dewi and his children, ridiculing their very genuine grief, but what the hell, it made him feel better.

'So how have you reacted since the funeral?' asked Ginnie, in a softer voice.

'Pretty bad, really. I've been very low.' He was surprised to find himself making the admission — it was not the kind of thing he'd ever said to her before — but at that moment it felt right.

'I'm not surprised. Because, whatever your feelings for Andrea have been since you split up, for a very long time you were in love with her.'

He shrugged. 'Well, I thought I was.'

'You were.'

'Yup. I thought I'd been part of a happy marriage . . . until Andrea told me how wrong I was.'

'I think she made your life pretty tough.'

'Oh, I don't know . . .' Why was he being so diffident? Was he conscious of the old taboo about 'speaking ill of the dead'?

'I saw you together a lot, Bill, and I

thought Andrea gave you a rough ride.'

'I don't think that's fair.' What strange instinct was it that that found him defending the woman who had rejected him?

'It may not be fair, but it's true. You have an exceptionally kind, gentle nature, and Andrea took advantage of that.'

'I'm not sure that —'

'Take my word for it, I'm right.'

He couldn't think what to say. After what he had been thinking about himself for the previous two weeks, to be told he had 'an exceptionally kind, gentle nature' came as something of a shock.

'You see, Bill, I never really liked Andrea.'

'I know, you said that. If you didn't like her, then why on earth did you stay in touch with us for so long?'

'It wasn't the "us" I wanted to stay in touch with, Bill. It was you.'

Again, Ginnie's words removed his capacity for speech. He could only gape at her, plastic tooth covers on display.

She reached forward once again to his hand. This time she did not place hers on top. She held his in a soft but firm grasp. 'You mean a lot to me, Bill. You have always meant a lot to me.'

He did manage to croak out, 'You mean a lot to me too, Ginnie.'

'And I think we ought to get together.'

'You and me?'

'There's no one else at the table, Bill.'

'No, but . . . Ginnie . . . I'm sorry, I'm not being very articulate.'

She shook his hand gently. 'You don't have to be.'

'But you . . . I always thought you were out of my league.'

' "Out of your league"? What on earth does that mean?'

'You're an internationally famous actress and I'm just a nonentity, an ex-newsreader who hasn't had much success at —'

'Bill, stop it. Don't put yourself down. All right, I've had a modicum of fame, but surely you've read enough in the tabloids to know that fame doesn't bring happiness. It takes you away from people, it puts a barrier between you and the rest of the world. It doesn't have any effect on who you love.'

She had used the word. Bill could not believe the way the evening was turning out. 'I've always loved you, Ginnie,' he said shyly.

'And I've always loved you.'

The rest of the meal flashed by. Bill knew what he was eating, because his order was always the same, but he tasted nothing. He and Ginnie were talking too much to be aware of food.

They talked about their childhoods, their families, subjects that had never come up during their brittle three-way conversations with Andrea, or even their more recent formal restaurant meetings. No time seemed to have passed when Bill became aware that they were the only people left in the place, and the waiter, looking significantly at his watch, smiled rather less benignly on Signor Stratton than he had earlier in the evening.

Outside the restaurant Bill and Ginnie joined together in a long kiss. Not hard, just gentle, teasing, exploratory.

'Not bad for someone with plastic veneers on,' she said, as they drew apart.

Bill felt suddenly clumsy, gauche, the adolescent on a date. 'I don't know if you fancy, er . . .' He'd never before invited a woman back, but . . . 'My flat's just round the corner. We could —'

Ginnie placed one finger gently on his lips. 'Not tonight, no.' Obviously he could not hide the disappointment in his face, because she went on, 'For purely practical reasons. The main one being that I'm still totally knackered and I've got a six o'clock make-up call for a shoot tomorrow morning. A commercial for a new Honey and Ginseng Health Drink, would you believe.' She smiled her famous smile. 'I want our first time to be special, don't you, Bill?'

'Yes,' he breathed.

'How's Saturday for you?'

'Good.'

'Come to my flat sevenish. I'll do dinner for you . . . amongst other things . . .'

'All right.' He grinned. 'And do you know what will have happened by then?'

'Surprise me.'

'I'll have my proper veneers in.'

'Excellent. We'll give them an appropriate christening on Saturday.'

They found her a cab. Another lingering kiss, full of adolescent anticipation, and she was gone.

Bill Stratton returned to his flat in a state of ecstasy. Unbelievable though it might seem, he was on a promise with Virginia Fairbrother.

Chapter twenty-three

. . . and, by way of contrast, a woman in Gateshead who was having difficulty selling her house offered 'A Night of Love' as an inducement to potential purchasers. The house is still on the market.

The day after his were fitted, Bill Stratton had lunch at the Turkish place with Sal to compare veneers. She was impressed and told him not to worry about the expense. He'd soon pay it off, because the cosmetic transformation would lead to a lot more work in front of camera.

She was still very pleased with her own veneers, but, Bill noticed, seemed set to discolour them as quickly as the originals they covered. She was smoking more than ever, even insisting on what she termed an 'intercourse cigarette' between their mezes and their mains.

'I thought you were giving up.'

'Yes, I was, Bill, but I've just read this book called *Deadly Sins: Six Out of Seven Can't Be Bad*. Its premise is that to avoid all seven is impossible, so choose one you really don't want to give up, stay with that and stop doing the others.'

'Sloth, Gluttony, Lust, Envy . . . I don't recall Smoking being one of the Deadly Sins.'

'No, the writer's redefined them for the twenty-first century.'

'Oh yes? What've they come up with?'

'Booze, Smoking, Doing Drugs, Screwing Around, Racial Intolerance, Road Rage and Obesity.'

'And you're only allowed to do one?'

'Yes. As you may have noticed, I chose Smoking.'

'So that means you've given up Screwing Around?'

'Chance'd be a fine thing. I haven't given up voluntarily.' She cocked a thoughtful brown eye at Bill. 'Funny we've never done that, isn't it?'

'What?'

'Screwed around. Shagged each other.' Apparently she reckoned he still looked uncomprehending. 'Been to bed together.'

'Yes, I did actually know what you meant.'

'Well, it is quite odd, isn't it? We've known each other a long time.'

'Sal, there are lots of people I've known for a long time who I haven't been to bed with. And I'm sure there are plenty like that in your life too.'

'Hmm . . .' She didn't sound so convinced that there were. 'Well, do you think we should try it one day?'

If she'd asked him that on any other occasion since the end of his marriage — except during his period of virtual mourning for Andrea — he'd have leapt at the chance. He always had found Sal attractive, and he couldn't forget the feeling of her body against his when he had told her that he loved her. Yes, on any other occasion he would have been urgently discussing the logistics of love — where and how soon.

On any other occasion, he thought with only a trace of wistfulness, as he treated her suggestion as if she'd been joking. But on this occasion he wasn't interested. He was on a promise with Virginia Fairbrother.

Thoughts of her filled his waking hours, which were extensive, because he didn't sleep a lot on the nights running up to the promised Saturday. Him and Ginnie . . . everything just seemed so logical. They had been meant for each other from way back. He still remembered the slight pang of lust when Andrea had first introduced him to 'her friend', that quickly-suppressed disappointed feeling that he hadn't got 'the pretty one'.

And, over the years, yes, he and Ginnie really had got on. The two of them had so much more in common, exchanging showbiz gossip, than they'd ever had with the conversations of Andrea and her NHS coven.

And to think Virginia Fairbrother had actually been holding a candle for him all this time . . . as soon as she told him that, he realised how big a candle he'd also been holding for her. And they'd both spent so many years hiding their lights under their individual bushels . . . God, they had a lot of time to make up.

There had been many occasions during his marriage when Bill and Ginnie had been alone together, but the thought had never occurred to him to make any advance towards her. Partly, he was faithful to Andrea, but also . . . well, he wasn't in Ginnie's league. And, besides, their relationship worked. Just friends. That way, nothing could stop them going on seeing each other forever. Nothing was broken, and nothing needed fixing.

Now he couldn't believe that he hadn't seen the logic of their being together earlier.

Virginia Fairbrother, though . . . imagine

turning up to a film première or a book launch with her on his arm, and letting the press know that they were an item. Bill Stratton had always been diffident about the press's interest in him. He didn't really think what he did was worthy of their attention. But as the partner of Virginia Fairbrother . . .

He was busy during that week, but the time still didn't go as quickly as it should have done. His final gluing session with the Australian cotton bud took quite a while. He had a couple of after-dinner speaking bookings, which once again he did on automatic pilot, though this time for reasons of excited preoccupation rather than alcoholic despair.

And on the Friday he paid his first visit to the BWOC office since Andrea's funeral. As he went through the door the mix of Carolyn's cigarette smoke and perfume was as safe and welcoming as ever.

She looked up from her computer, for once surprised by his arrival. No reference to 'the big boss'. 'Are you okay?' she asked.

'Fine.' Wouldn't anyone be fine if they knew they were going to be making love to Virginia Fairbrother the following day?

'It's just . . . you seemed so upset at the funeral . . . and you haven't returned my calls and I was worried about you . . .'

Bless your little heart, thought Bill. I've never heard you sound less cynical. 'That's very kind of you, Carolyn, to think of me. Yes, I was very down for a few weeks —'

'Did you keep smoking?'

'No, I didn't. Drank a bit too much, but no ciggies. Though I would still like to thank you for the one you gave me after the funeral. It was precisely what I needed at the time.'

'My pleasure. But you're feeling better now, are you?'

I am actually — for reasons that I can't possibly tell you — feeling on top of the world. But all he said was, 'Yes. I was very down for a few weeks, but then I thought . . . hell, life goes on.'

'Doesn't it bloody just?' said Carolyn, instantly resuming her customary tough exterior.

'Anyway, reason I'm here . . . I did a couple of after-dinner gigs this week and, you know, I've been doing the same lines for so long that I'm sick to death of them. I thought maybe I'd interpolate some new ones.'

'That's bold, changing a winning formula.'

'I'm feeling bold at the moment.'

'Good for you, Bill.' Her blue eyes gazed quizzically at his. 'What's got into you then . . . ?' She could never resist the obvious innuendo. 'Or should I ask what you've been getting into?'

Oh, if you only knew . . . but he gave her some reply about having got over the shock of the funeral and feeling more positive by the minute. Then he asked if she'd had any good 'by way of contrast' lines in recently.

'A few.' She shuffled through the papers on her desk. Bill was once again aware of the luxurious curves of her back. Carolyn really was a very attractive woman. He felt very warm towards her. Part of him wanted to reach out and touch her. He might even have suggested their going out for a drink . . . if he hadn't been on a promise with Virginia Fairbrother.

'I quite like this.' She proffered a sheet of paper.

Bill took it and read, ' "A giantess in a Ukrainian circus married the company midget, but then divorced him because he didn't come up to her expectations." Very good. Funny, a lot of the recent ones read more like made-up jokes than genuine news stories. Still, it just goes to show that truth is stranger than fiction . . . and various other such platitudes . . .' He passed the paper back. 'Could you print me out a list of . . . I don't know, say twenty of the new ones you think are up to standard and email them to me? Then, next time I'm doing a gig and think of a new one, I'll try slipping it in.'

'Yes, I've heard that about you.'

It took him a moment to recognise the *double entendre*. 'God, I do set them up for you, don't I? Should have learned not to do it by now 'cause we've known each other . . . how long is it?'

'You tell me,' said Carolyn, with an enigmatic, almost insolent smile.

Virginia Fairbrother had a house in Docklands, backing on to the Thames. In her fifties, she had benefited from one of those recurrent phases when Hollywood fell in love with British character actors. She'd had a lot of supporting roles in some very bad films and a couple of half-decent ones. Those had paid for the house.

Bill had been there before a few times. The house-warming party had taken place while he was still unsuspectingly married to Andrea, and they had gawped at the gallery of showbiz stars who had graced the occasion. He thought they'd both had a really good time, but in the taxi back to Putney Andrea had gone on about all the people there being 'false' and 'artificial' and 'not engaging with the real world'.

But he'd never before approached Ginnie's house feeling as he did that Saturday night. As ever, punctual to the point of being early, he had asked the cab to drop him a couple of streets away, and dawdled towards the door, reckoning ten past seven would be about right for her 'sevenish'. Not so late as to appear casually uncaring, nor so early as to look puppyishly eager . . . though that was how he felt.

He rang the doorbell, new veneers gleaming, heart pounding with a fizzing cocktail of emotions. There was excitement close to ecstasy, and almost unbearable lust, both swept along on an undercurrent of anxiety. The last time he'd made love to a woman . . . or to be more accurate, the last time he had failed to make love to a woman . . . had been that final night with Leigh.

When she opened the door, Ginnie took his breath away. She had always looked wonderful, but never like this. Her skin, still tanned from Croatia, glowed through a simple full-length dress in the finest white linen with a vaguely Arabic cut. The auburn hair, which had grown a little since the filming ended, was skilfully spiked, half Peter Pan, half street urchin. And her jewellery that night was silver; light filigree necklace and bracelets, dangling earrings as insubstantial as spiders' webs.

A musky, smoky perfume enveloped Bill as she leant forward to kiss him and led him into the candle-lit Aladdin's cave behind her. Music billowed around them. Mozart almost definitely. A Clarinet Concerto perhaps.

Their kiss had been formal, almost perfunctory, as if they both knew there was no hurry. The ending of the evening was preordained, there was no urgency, they could luxuriate in heady anticipation.

She had champagne opened and on ice. They drank easily, not to excess, and the liquor worked its age-old relaxing magic. The food she produced was perfect, very light. Little filo pastry pies of cheese and spinach, tiny courgette fritters, and dips of spicy vegetables prepared them for the beautifully glazed cold salmon with delicately buttered new potatoes and subtly piquant salad that followed. Whether Ginnie had assembled this feast herself or bought it in Bill did not know. Nor did he care.

They didn't move on to another wine. They continued to drink champagne.

And they talked, again without pressure, inconsequentially, subjects constantly varying, as they do between two people who care for each other, and have been friends for a long time.

Bill had been worried about the transition from dining room to bedroom, but he need not have done. He was in the hands of an expert stage manager. As soon as he had refused her offer of coffee, Ginnie disappeared into the kitchen and returned moments later with a newly-opened bottle of champagne. Elegantly scooping up their two glasses as she passed, she announced easily, 'I think it's time we went upstairs.'

She pointed out a guest bathroom to him, but Bill didn't need it.

'Come through to the bedroom then. I'll just use my bathroom.'

'And what do I do the while?'

She grinned at him. 'You could do worse than take all your clothes off and get into bed.'

The bedroom had not been neglected by the punctilious stage management. The walls were rich terracotta, lit by the tremor of many candles. White muslin flowed down from a central point over the big white bed, which faced large windows shielding a balcony that looked out over the Thames. An almost silent procession of Saturday night pleasure boats animated the view.

From the largest, a brightly-lit party vessel, the sound of a distant jazz band filtered through into Virginia Fairbrother's eyrie. The air was redolent of musk and rose petals.

Bill Stratton sat on a chair and removed his shoes. Then, as instructed, he took off his clothes. He folded them neatly on the chair, and slipped under the duvet. He went to the right, the side he had always occupied during his marriage to Andrea. The pile of books on the left-hand table suggested he had made the right decision. A propitious omen, he hoped.

As he lay there, breathing in the scent of Ginnie's sheets, he still had difficulty in believing the journey that he had travelled since Andrea's death.

The door from the bathroom opened softly, and she came towards him. She was not yet naked, but wore a flimsy gown of oyster grey silk, tied loosely at the waist, showing a long v of brown flesh above her waist and yards of brown leg below.

'Bill, I'm glad to see you've made yourself at home.'

She slipped easily into the left-hand side of the bed. Their eyes engaged. Then gently, almost ceremoniously, they kissed.

'Well, this has been a long time coming,'

murmured Ginnie.

'Better late than never,' murmured Bill.

He reached a hand to run along the ridge of her shoulder. It was hard, almost un-yielding. His hand slipped down her back over the silk to rest on the curve of her bottom. That too felt hard, toned almost to the rigidity of plastic.

Her thin hands played down his sides, teasing, touching, ever downward. His body responded, but he felt nothing.

There was a numbness, an awkwardness. Their bodies seemed incongruously the wrong shape, never designed to lock to-gether, like a metal puzzle out of a Christmas cracker. Where all should be softness and melting, all was edges and dry-ness.

Neither one of them voiced the thought, but they both knew it wasn't working. Bill wasn't impotent, but his erection felt like what the word suggested, a mechanical hy-draulic piece of apparatus. A level of pene-tration was achieved, he even had a kind of orgasm, though Ginnie's claim to have done the same — brilliant actress though she was — didn't fool either of them.

The experience was unlike anything Bill Stratton had previously encountered. It felt about as natural as a stick insect trying to make love to . . . not even another stick insect, but a stick.

Basically, it was bad sex. He and Ginnie had never been designed to be more than good friends.

After about an hour of purposeless grinding, they both started an elaborate sequence of yawns. Goodness, Ginnie didn't realise how tired she still was after the filming in Croatia. Goodness, Bill was still pretty wiped out from the couple of after-dinner speaking engagements he'd done that week.

Well, they'd both got to an age when they needed their sleep, and they wouldn't sleep so well with an unfamiliar partner and . . . Ginnie did not demur when Bill said maybe he'd better be on his way. He put his clothes back on as quickly as he could, filling the silence by passing platitudinous comments about the shipping on the Thames.

He was desperate to leave now, desperate to be in a cab on his way back to Pimlico. Ginnie was equally desperate for him to go.

But, of course, neither of them put their desperation into words.

Instead, they both agreed it had been wonderful. They both agreed that they should do it again, soon.

And they both knew that they never would.

Chapter twenty-four

. . . and, by way of contrast, a man in Lewes announced that he'd given up sex because he found Morris Dancing more exciting.

'A strange thing happened last night.'

'Oh,' said Carolyn. 'What?'

'I did an after-dinner speaking gig, and a guy came up afterwards and said he'd heard most of my "by way of contrast" lines before.'

'So? He had a long memory. He'd heard them while you were still being a newsreader.'

'No, couldn't be that. Because most of the lines I used last night were recent ones. You know, I said I was going to get some new stuff into the routine.'

'Oh yes?' Carolyn took a long draw on her cigarette, almost as if she was trying to prevent herself from laughing. But it couldn't be that, Bill reasoned. There was nothing in his current situation to laugh at.

'Anyway, I got quite cross with this bloke. He was treating me as if I was just some second-rate stand-up comic, recycling old material.'

'You are recycling old material.'

'Yes, I know I am. But the material I am recycling is not just old jokes. They are all genuine news stories. I mean, what I do does have some journalistic integrity.'

' "Journalistic integrity"? That sounds a bit pompous coming from you, Bill.'

'I know it does. But this guy really got me riled. I nearly lost my temper with him.'

'Oh dear. That's unlike you. Has something happened recently in your life to shorten your . . . famously long fuse?' As so often with Carolyn, there was an ambiguous impudence in her look, both aware and innocent of the potential innuendo.

'No,' Bill replied grumpily. Though almost a week had passed since his encounter with Ginnie, he still felt raw and embarrassed. But he wasn't going to let on about that to Carolyn.

He looked across at her, and now there was no doubt. Something was really amusing her. She was having great difficulty in suppressing her giggles.

'What is it?'

She sighed regretfully. 'Oh, I suppose I've got to come clean.'

'About what?'

'The whole BWOC thing.'

'Yes . . . ?'

'The "by way of contrast" lines have *always* been of dubious origin.'

'How do you mean?'

'A lot of them are almost urban myths, the kind of stories that get passed around in pubs.'

'All right. I'll buy that. And therein lies a lot of their appeal.'

'Yes.' She sighed again. The telling wasn't proving quite as easy as she had thought. 'Look, you know Jason has done a lot of work for BWOC —'

'Of course. Without him we wouldn't have the website. He's set up our whole computer system.'

'Actually, Bill, he's done rather more than that.'

He stared at her, uncomprehending.

'Do I have to spell it out?'

'I rather think you do.'

'All right.' Carolyn took a long, fortifying pull from her cigarette. 'Bill, you know Jason's setting himself up as a stand-up and comedy writer . . . ?'

'Yes, you told me.'

'Since he's been doing that, he's also been employed by BWOC.'

'I know that. We pay him a retainer to maintain the computer systems.'

'No. He's also been employed by BWOC

as a writer. A comedy writer.'

Finally, the penny dropped. 'You mean that all the recent "by way of contrast" lines . . . haven't been culled from international news agencies . . . they've all been invented . . . by Jason?'

Ruefully, Carolyn nodded her blonde head. 'I'm sorry. He needed the work and . . .' For the first time since Bill had met her, she looked abashed. 'I suppose I'd better resign, hadn't I?'

There was a long silence while Bill worked out his reactions to the news. Part of him was angry about having been duped. But another part of him relished the warm atmosphere of the BWOC office with Carolyn inside it. The prospect of someone else taking over the role was a bleak one.

'I don't think you need to do that,' he said eventually.

'What?' There was genuine relief in her voice, even the glistening of a tear in her eye.

'All you have to do —' Bill grinned broadly.

'Is what?'

'Tell your son to write better jokes.'

'But, Bill, what about your "journalistic integrity"?'

'Oh, sod that.'

'I knew you'd come round eventually,' said Trevor.

'Come round to what?'

'The end of sex.'

'I wouldn't say I've done that.'

'Listen, from what you've told me — and granted, you haven't given me a great deal of detail, but you implied a lot — you have recently had a disappointment in the bedroom department.'

'Well . . .'

'Don't deny it. I think it's put you off women.'

'Maybe temporarily.'

'There's no "temporarily" at our stage in life, Bill. Use it or lose it. Like old squash-players who leave the game for a couple of years and then try and come back to it. That's when they get the coronaries. No, you could well have given up sex for good, old son.'

Bill thought about what Trevor had said. Yes, it was entirely possible that his excruciating fumbling with Ginnie had been the last time he would ever make love. The experience had rather put him off the whole idea.

Had it been the last time, though? And if it had, surely such a rite of passage deserved some kind of recognition? What is an appropriate celebration, he wondered, for the last time in your life that you make love? Tricky, actually. Because only people who take religious vows or approach radical surgery actually know with certainty which the last time is. For the rest of us, we always wish that we'll get lucky just one more time . . . and hopefully a good few more.

There's a kind of Micawberism in sex. We always hope that something will turn up.

And one day, finally, something won't turn up, and we'll know that the shutter — always imagined to be ten years away in the mists of the future — has finally come down. And what will we have to look forward to then?

Bill Stratton shook such gloomy thoughts out of his head and picked up their beer glasses. 'We need a couple more of these. And when we've got them, we'll drink a toast.'

'What to?'

'You had the words for it, Trevor. "The end of sex".'

'See? I told you you'd come round to the idea.'

And, as Bill crossed to The Annexe's gloomy bar, he felt comforted. Trevor was right. It would be a monumental relief never to think about women or sex again.

'I don't see that it matters at all.'

'But, Sal, I am kind of passing them off as genuine news stories.'

'So who cares about that? You won't be the first after-dinner speaker to have used a scriptwriter. Read the back of *Private Eye* — you'd be amazed the number of people offering to customise speeches for special occasions.'

'No, I suppose it's all right. I just, sort of . . . feel that I'm selling myself under false pretences.'

'We all do that. There are whole industries which do nothing else. Public Relations, for one.'

'I suppose so.'

Sal's anxious navy-blue eyes sought his. 'Does it really worry you, Bill?'

He chuckled. 'No, I can't really say it does. I've always been full of shit. I'm just now full of more shit than I realised.' He ate a mouthful of his Iskender kebab and swilled it down with a glass of the old Yakut, before saying, 'You know, I think you were right, Sal.'

'I'm right so much of the time, you're going to have to narrow it down.'

'You told me that I was angry after the break-up with Andrea, and I denied it. But her death has made me realise just how right you were.'

'I won't say, "Told you so".'

'You don't have to. I know. I thought the bad treatment I got from Andrea justified my bad behaviour to other women. She had hurt me, so I took it out on them. I remember, you said that's what I was doing. You'd read it in some book, called *Anger: Men at Work*, I think it was?'

'No, it was actually in *Throttling the Individual: an Analysis of Marriage*.'

'Whatever . . .'

'And the point is reinforced in a new book I've just read, called *You Are What You Hate*. You should read it some day.'

'I can't see that day ever coming.'

'Hmm. It's a pity you don't read stuff like that, Bill.'

'Why?'

'Because you have such a poor understanding of your own personality.'

'My personality isn't that interesting.'

'Don't you believe it. Everyone's personality is interesting.'

'Maybe. So, anyway, you don't think I should stop doing the after-dinner speaking?'

'Good heavens, no. Why on earth do you ask that?'

'Well, because I now know that the "by way

of contrast" lines are all made up. It makes me feel, kind of . . . trivial and shallow.'

'Bill, your triviality and shallowness are what make you attractive.'

'Ah . . . well, all right.' Had Sal actually ever said before that he was attractive? He couldn't remember.

'I heard, incidentally,' she said, rather more serious now, 'that you've been seen around more with Virginia Fairbrother . . .'

He blushed, as if Sal had actually witnessed the bedroom scene in Docklands. 'Yes, she's always been a good friend of mine.'

'Hmm. No more than that? You're not an item?'

'Good God, no.' Was it fanciful to think that Sal had seemed relieved by his answer?

'So you're not currently an item with anyone?'

'No. I think I've probably already caused enough destruction in the world of relationships. I'm giving up women.'

'Really?'

'Yes.'

'Oh.'

'And what does that deflated little "Oh" mean?'

'Just that . . . for you to give up women, Bill . . . well, it'd be an awful waste . . .'

Chapter twenty-five

. . . and, by way of contrast, after an open-air Shakespeare production was rained off at the interval, a party of schoolchildren went home convinced that 'Romeo and Juliet' had a happy ending.

It is to be hoped that no one goes to their grave without having had at least one experience of perfect sex.

Perfect sex cannot be measured by any external values or criteria. It concerns only the two people involved. (Some authorities maintain that more than two people can be involved in perfect sex, but the general view is that, while extra partners may add to the physical sensation, they are unlikely to achieve the mental harmony that can exist between two participants.)

Nor are there any rules for what constitutes perfect sex. There is no manual available listing the required positions, no phrase book spelling out the required words. Perfect sex is instinctive; it is a happy coincidence of two complementary instincts, which will only be recognised by those who have been fortunate enough to experience it.

And perfect sex is almost always recognised on a first encounter. The sex on that first encounter may not be perfect — how often is sex on a first encounter perfect? — but it holds the potential for perfection.

Of course perfect sex has nothing to do with what the participants look like. Most members of the human race are, viewed objectively, pretty ugly. But that doesn't mean that nobody's going to love them. And an ongoing love, which is the best sort — though not achieved by everyone — is surely not going to be put off by the odd wrinkle, stretchmark or blue spider's web of veins. Skin's still skin, and nothing will ever replace the warm feel of it.

And in perfect sex, skin recognises skin. The excitement of the new is mixed with a feeling of ancient, atavistic familiarity. Two bodies cease to be awkward assemblages of limbs and imperfections. Their responses join forces with the mutual — and sole — aim of bestowing pleasure.

The minds meld too. Inhibitions, prohibitions, anxieties, vanities, suspicions and jealousies melt away in the sheer glee of two bodies. Perfect sex is very simple. Nothing has ever felt so natural. And it holds at bay the fear of death. During perfect sex, the participants are going to live for ever.

Time stops.

As it stopped for Bill and Carolyn the first time they made love.

Chapter twenty-six

. . . and, by way of contrast, a catwalk model in Nigeria has successfully sued a tabloid newspaper for describing her as 'thin'.

Nothing could have been more casual. Even though the whole premise of the BWOC — and Bill's tenuous claim to 'journalistic integrity' — had been blown out of the water, he had seen no reason to close the office down. There was still demand for 'by way of contrast' lines as newspaper fillers from all over the world, and the fact that they were mostly spurious inventions by Jason didn't seem to matter. All jokes undergo metamorphosis as they are disseminated. The 'me' to whom 'a funny thing happened' is never the comedian telling the joke. He's heard it from someone else, who heard it from someone else, who . . . and so on down an endless corridor of reflecting and distorting mirrors.

Even the jokes that start from true stories get embroidered and customised in the telling. The phrasing can always be improved, the word order adjusted to get the pay-off at the end. After all that treatment, who really cares whether the story started off as real life or was the fabrication of a skilled scriptwriter?

Bill Stratton certainly didn't.

The other reason he was unwilling to close down the BWOC operation was that the business gave him a legitimate reason to keep seeing Carolyn. Except for an awareness of her 'obvious sexuality', he wouldn't have said that he particularly fancied her. Her wonderful, voluptuous curves seemed perhaps too rich, a Black Forest Gâteau of a body. But he enjoyed sharing the cocoon of her presence, that shelter of Radio 2, cigarette smoke, sweet tea and biscuits.

He'd dropped in to the BWOC office one morning, some three months after the Virginia Fairbrother debacle. (He and Ginnie had talked on the phone the day after, and agreed they were both looking forward to the next time they met. Neither mentioned the sex. And, in spite of occasional short calls, their diaries hadn't yet found mutual windows to arrange another dinner at another newly-opened restaurant. But, of course, as they kept saying, they would soon.)

The morning he went to see Carolyn, Bill Stratton was feeling his age. In spite of its gleaming veneers, the face that had looked out of the shaving mirror that morning was the face of his father on his deathbed. Life was ticking on. Sal kept the PAs and after-dinner speaking bookings coming in, but there was a sameness to everything Bill did. Soon he would have to decide whether his remaining years would spiral slowly downwards doing more of the same; or whether he still had in him the potential for one more change or adventure. He really was in the Penultimate Chance Saloon.

Maybe it was this feeling of doom that made him behave differently that morning. After the usual combative banter with Carolyn, realising it was about time he should be on his way, and seeing the day stretching endlessly ahead of him, he had said — before he had time to think about what he was saying, 'Do you fancy slipping out for a bit of lunch?'

Not one of his repertoire of posh restaurants. Just a grubby pub round the corner. They ate Steak and Guinness pie. He drank pints of bitter. Carolyn ordered something the very idea of which repelled him; Bailey's Irish Cream. Bailey's, and Steak and Guinness Pie! But that's what she wanted, and that's what he ordered for her.

If asked afterwards, Bill couldn't have

said exactly what they talked about over that smoky lunch. Certainly nothing to do with BWOC. And he certainly didn't try to entertain her with any 'by way of contrast' lines. Of all the women in the world, Carolyn was never going to be seduced by those. She already knew every one of them. So Bill's enduring conversational defence was totally dismantled. He had to talk about himself.

All he could remember of their conversation was that it felt entirely natural.

Neither could remember which one of them had suggested going back to his flat.

But that too had felt entirely natural.

Chapter twenty-seven

. . . and, by way of contrast, a Manchester travel company are advertising September discounts on their Greek villas, all complete with swimming pool and a car thrown in.

They were on loungers beside the pool, frying slowly in the Greek sun. The bar was only a few metres away, but the effort of going to get a cool beer was insuperable. Never mind, the waiter would do his rounds in a moment.

Bill knew he should really put on some more suntan lotion, but that again seemed too much like hard work.

The block of the hotel towered above them. Soon they'd drift into the taverna area for lunch. That night they'd booked for a 'Greek Evening' in the restaurant, audience participation dancing, smashing plates, the lot.

The hotel was a complete 'tourist trap', and Bill Stratton loved it.

He loved Carolyn too. The body beside his was perhaps too bulky to wear a bikini, but who actually cared? He loved every contour of it.

Andrea had always said that Carolyn had 'an obvious sexuality'. But what the hell was wrong with the obvious?

They'd been together nearly six months. Though precisely who'd made the first move was confused in their memories, they were both ecstatic that it had happened.

At first Bill had escorted her to restaurants and then back to bed in Pimlico, but Carolyn wanted more than that. Confining the scenes of his encounters to restaurants and bedrooms, making choices from one menu or the other, had always kept Bill at a distance from the women he was with. Carolyn wanted a relationship that encroached into other rooms. Champagne was all very well, but daily life was sustained by cups of tea. Carolyn craved a degree of domesticity.

And Bill was unable to refuse her anything she wanted. After two months, she had moved into the Pimlico flat. When they got back from their fortnight on Corfu, they would actively start looking for somewhere bigger.

Till then, they would enjoy the sun and the idleness and the love-making. Bill still kept asking himself how he could have known Carolyn for so long and not realised how stunning she would be in bed. She enjoyed their intimacy at least as much as he did. The previous night she had promised that they would 'go on making love like this until the Zimmer frames get in the way too much.'

And the night before that, when too many post-prandial Greek brandies had taken their toll on his performance, she had said, 'Just have a cuddle. It'll come back.'

Never had impotence felt so intimate.

Now he was with Carolyn, Bill Stratton had reached a kind of maturity at the end of his second adolescence. He was happier than he'd ever dared expect he might be.

There were a few clouds on his horizon, but only small ones. Having seen Andrea's diminished state in hospital, he worried about Carolyn's smoking. But she'd maintained the habit since her early teens and showed no signs of giving up. If he ever raised the subject, he got a strong response about it being her life and up to her what she did with it. So now he never raised the subject.

But the anxiety remained.

He was also aware of his own age, more aches and twinges every day when he got up, his white hair thinning, and the knowledge that he'd be lucky to have twenty more years. But there was a peaceful inevitability about it. Bill Stratton smiled a lot, flashing his crooked smile of veneered teeth.

The lives of worthy heroes have worthy resolutions, but less admirable men can also make journeys towards self-knowledge. Though they're lesser journeys, they still count. And Bill Stratton had made such a journey.

And what had he learnt from it? Well, one thing. Something that a man with more sense of his own importance might have dignified with the title 'Bill Stratton's Law of Relationships'. Very simple, really. 'If the sex doesn't work, get out.' The idea that bad sex will eventually transmute into good sex is — like that other recurrent belief in gender negotiations, that a woman can change a man — entirely fallacious.

He leant across in his lounger towards Carolyn. Her eyes, which had been closed, sensed his scrutiny and opened, their familiar blueness deeper from the reflection of the Greek sky.

'I just wanted to say,' Bill murmured, 'that I've never felt closer to another human being.'

'It's mutual,' her husky, cigarette-roughened voice replied.

'I want us to be together forever.'

'Mutual too.'

He felt an urge to say more, a recurrent urge which always wanted to say the same thing. He was divorced and, as if to reinforce his lack of commitments, his ex-wife was dead. Carolyn, he had soon established, was long divorced from Jason's father. They were two grown-ups without ties, who wanted to spend the rest of their lives together. There was a strong logic about what he should say next, and he knew he had in his power the ability to make Carolyn very happy.

He leant across and kissed her, soft responsive lips.

Bill Stratton had witnessed enough mushy films to know what was expected of him at this point. He felt the words once again forming on his lips, Will you marry me? That's what he should say.

But then he stopped and thought. He thought of all the times through his life when he'd done what he should. It was the 'should' imperative that had made him marry Andrea, and had kept him faithful to her for so long. A different 'should' had fuelled his burst of late-onset promiscuity — the feeling he was having all the women he should have had much earlier. And now that in Carolyn he'd got the one woman he wanted and the woman he wanted to spend

340

the rest of his life with, he felt a surging sense of freedom. And as to the thought of marrying her, he felt a gleeful, childish, instinctive response:

Why should I?

We hope you have enjoyed this Large Print book. Other Thorndike, Wheeler or Chivers Press Large Print books are available at your library or directly from the publishers.

For more information about current and upcoming titles, please call or write, without obligation, to:

Publisher
Thorndike Press
295 Kennedy Memorial Drive
Waterville, ME   04901
Tel. (800) 223-1244

Or visit our Web site at:
www.thomson.com/thorndike
www.thomson.com/wheeler

OR

Chivers Large Print
published by BBC Audiobooks Ltd
St James House, The Square
Lower Bristol Road
Bath BA2 3BH
England
Tel. +44(0) 800 136919
email: bbcaudiobooks@bbc.co.uk
www.bbcaudiobooks.co.uk

All our Large Print titles are designed for easy reading, and all our books are made to last.